Dorothy Parker's

TELEPHONE ME NOW

FIVE, TEN, FIFTEEN, TWENTY…

Selected Stories from the 2018
Literary Taxidermy Short Story Competition

Edited by

MARK MALAMUD

TELEPHONE ME NOW

All stories © 2018 by their respective authors
Introduction © 2018 by Mark Malamud
Anthology © 2018 by Regulus Press
Cover art (detail from "Tax Poetic") © 2018 by Andy Eccleshall

First Regulus Press printing November 2018
Signal Library 30-8102-71-01

Regulus Press, Seattle WA
www.regulus.press

ISBN: 0999446223
ISBN-13: 978-0999446225
(Regulus Press)

OPPORTUNITIES FOR
FUTURE TAXIDERMY

"A story has no beginning or end; arbitrarily one chooses that moment of experience from which to look back or from which to look ahead. I'm too tired and old to learn to love, leave me alone for ever."
— GRAHAM GREENE, *THE END OF THE AFFAIR*

"One beast and only one howls in the woods by night. See! sweet and sound she sleeps in granny's bed, between the paws of the tender wolf."
— ANGELA CARTER, "THE COMPANY OF WOLVES"

"I have never seen anything like it: two little discs of glass suspended in front of his eyes in loops of wire. This is not the scene I dreamed of."
— J. M. COETZEE, *WAITING FOR THE BARBARIANS*

"It was a pleasure to burn. When we reach the city."
— RAY BRADBURY, *FAHRENHEIT 451*

"Suddenly Denton realized that there would be three of them, that they would come after dark, that their leader would have his own key, and that they would be calm and deliberate, confident that they had all the time they needed to do what had to be done. The leader held his hand firmly as life poured away, and Denton's death began."
— MARTIN AMIS, "DENTON'S DEATH"

"He could have shouted and could not. They found her caressing his wild dead hair."
— SAMUEL BECKETT, "ASSUMPTION"

"On our wedding day I was forty-six, she was eighteen. And we rode forward into the night, past the sleeping houses of our countrymen."
— GEORGE SANDERS, *LINCOLN IN THE BARDO*

"Lesser catching sight of himself in the lonely glass wakes to finish his book. Mercy mercy"
— BERNARD MALAMUD, *THE TENANTS*

"Katy drives like a maniac; we must have been doing over 120 kilometers per hour on those turns. For-A-While."
— JOANNA RUSS, "WHEN IT CHANGED"

Please, God, let him telephone me now.
↓
Five, ten, fifteen, twenty, twenty-five, thirty, thirty-five.

— Dorothy Parker, first and last line from "A Telephone Call"

CONTENTS

Introduction

Welcome to *Telephone Me Now*, one of three anthologies that collect the prize-winning stories from the 2018 Literary Taxidermy Short Story Competition.

Literary taxidermy is a story-writing process that involves taking the first and last sentence from a well-known work (often a novel, but sometimes a short story) and then "re-stuffing" what goes in-between those lines to create a new, wholly-original narrative. The goal of the literary taxidermist is not just to slap someone else's words onto the start and finish of an otherwise stand-alone story, but to take full ownership of the borrowed lines, interpreting (or re-interpreting) them in order to make them seamless, integral, and in fact the *perfect* start and finish for the new story being told.

The origin of literary taxidermy is *The Gymnasium*, a collection of nineteen stories written between 2003 and 2017 that "re-stuff" classic works by Milan Kundera, Thomas Wolfe, Ian Fleming, and others. The earliest stories started as little more than a casual prompted-writing exercise, a quick & dirty way to keep my hands busy between other, larger projects. The twist of providing both a start and finish as part of the prompt wasn't deeply considered. I am a believer in creative parsimony, also known as laziness, and so the idea of leveraging the words of another writer in this way seemed both simple and convenient. There was a certain novelty, to be sure; but there's novelty in throwing open cans of paint against a canvas, too. It might seem like a good idea at the time — it might in fact *be* a good idea at the time — who doesn't enjoy a moment of chaotic release? — but that doesn't mean you end up with anything worthwhile.

But I got lucky.

It turned out there was something surprisingly satisfying about working within this particular delimited structure, balancing appropriation and originality, managing another's voice and my own, and charting a new path to a known destination. Very quickly those "other, larger projects" fell aside. My quick & dirty exercise had become a full-time obsession. Many stories followed.

During those early days, my curiosity was focused on where each pair of first and last lines (some of them with quite well-known trajectories) would take *me*; but that changed when — about halfway through what would become *The Gymnasium* — I enjoined several other writers to co-participate in my literary experiment. We'd each take the same first/last lines, go off for a week or two, then return to compare our efforts. The results — "sibling stories" we called them — made me realize that there was another collection I wanted to see: a book composed entirely of stories that all start and end the same way, but written by different authors.

Which brings us to the anthology you hold in your hands and the competition that produced it.

The Literary Taxidermy Short Story Competition, sponsored by Regulus Press, invites writers to stitch together their own stories using the opening and closing sentences of classic works of fiction. For the 2018 competition, aspiring writers were given three choices: *The Thin Man* by Dashiell Hammett; *Through the Looking-Glass* by Lewis Carroll; or "A Telephone Call" by Dorothy Parker.

The present anthology contains stories from the Parker contest. That means that every story you're about to read starts and ends *exactly* the same way — with the first and last sentence of the short story "A Telephone Call" by Dorothy Parker. Of course *the path* that each author takes from beginning to end is unique — and therein lies a particular thrill of reading these short works: despite sharing a common frame, they are all *different*.

So some of the stories in this collection are serious, some are humorous, some are conceptual, some are disturbing, and some are just *strange*. They cross genres; they cross continents (and occasionally cross into the future); and they vary in style and diction and tone and voice. Reading each one is like getting a peek at the results of someone else's Rorschach test.

The authors are eclectic, too. They range in age from eighteen to — well, I'm not sure how old the oldest is, but probably at least as old as I am. (And I'm *old*.) They also span the globe, so you're about to read stories from the United States, Canada, Australia, New Zealand, and the UK. (And that's why you may notice stories written in British and American English — so don't be shocked to find *colour* in one story and *color* in the next.) The winning author in this year's Parker contest is Nina Kaushikkar, an eighteen-year-old American student from Illinois. Her story "Usha's Sarees" examines the thread of tradition as it weaves through modernity. It is both bittersweet and beautiful.

But there's more to these stories than the pleasure found in their distinction or their differences. Their *similarities* can be just as intriguing.

Yes, you will find a number of stories within this collection that are about desperation — after all, the opening line is *Please, God, let him telephone me now.*

And the last line — *Five, ten, fifteen, twenty, twenty-five, thirty, thirty-five.* — guarantees there are numerous tales obsessed with counting.

But *those* similarities are not particularly interesting. What's interesting are the similarities that appear in story after story that are *unexpected*. For example, this contest received a statistically-improbable number of stories that include dead fathers, school shootings, and pencil skirts. Why? What is it about *those* two lines by Dorothy Parker that trigger *these* particular narrative neurons to fire?

Literary taxidermy is nothing if not a kind of inkblot test, an invitation to interpret and then riff inside an ambiguous narrative frame. Even if the bizarre similarities that emerge are inexplicable (and really: why *do* so many of the Parker stories concern contract killers?), it shouldn't be a shock that the same input yields similar output. And yet the black box in-between — the human imagination — remains a mystery.

I really had no idea what to expect when Regulus Press launched this competition, but in the end I was amazed and inspired by the enthusiasm of the response. The stories in all three anthologies (this one, as well as *Against the Bar* and *One Thing Was Certain* for the Hammett and Carroll contests) were selected anonymously by myself, the editors at Regulus Press, and a panel of eight professional-writer judges. The stories are entertaining, intriguing, and occasionally shocking. After each story, you'll find a short biographical note about the author, and maybe — just maybe — *you* can figure out how they ended up writing the story they did!

Mark Malamud
3 October 2018

Everything After

PLEASE, GOD, let him telephone me now.

He remembers thinking it. It seems like so long ago at this point — ages, lifetimes. It may as well have been.

He moved to this country to get a fresh start. He wanted to experience something new, find love, find himself. *He did*; but his heart breaks with the realization that *this* is where life was always meant to lead him.

Why is the brain even capable of conjuring such dreams? Why did God allow us to hope and imagine something more for ourselves if he had already determined our fate before our first cells were ever formed?

These are the things he thinks about now.

These are the thoughts that keep him up at night — not that he sleeps much now anyway.

It used to be easier.

He used to be ignorant.

Those were the days. The blissful, simple, wonderful days. Back when he first stepped off that plane onto that tarmac. He coughed with his first breath of that muggy, New York air, but he didn't mind. The tall buildings waved at him from the distance, and he grinned — *this was it*.

That would be the start of it all … his new beginning.

The nice lady at customs told him that she liked his accent.

Some young, black boys were spinning themselves atop a piece of cardboard on the corner just outside the airport. Their bright clothes and tall hair mirrored the vibrant city.

Their music popped and snapped up the endless concrete walks. He was mesmerized; so much so, that he almost missed his cab.

The cab driver that picked him up said that he liked his accent too — at least, that's what he thought the man said; but the driver's own accent was so thick and foreign, he couldn't really be certain. The only thing he was certain of was the price of the fare once they reached the hotel; and with his pockets a lot lighter, he walked inside to book a room.

He spent the next week just trying to get his bearings. The streets seemed to be a mass of grey, sticky, spider webs, and the natives moved along the strings like they were nothing, knocking around the poor, pathetic fly that he was whenever he got in their way. But eventually — with time, with effort, all that began to change.

He learned the ins and outs of the city. The alleyways and flashing lights from the cars, the billboards, the rush of the bike messengers in the dead of night — they became familiar to him. Inviting.

Exciting.

He was an Englishman in America.

He was the old in the new.

And even though he was only twenty five, *here* — he felt younger somehow. Walking those dirty streets, listening to the loonies preach about love in the subway cars, seeing the reflection of himself in the sides of the buildings — he *looked* younger. He looked good.

And Darius thought so too.

A beautiful boy with beautiful, dark skin, and eyes that almost looked purple in the steamy air at the base of the city — *this* beautiful boy saw a beautiful boy within *him*; and it didn't take long after they met for the two of them to get tangled up atop that ratty couch in his studio apartment. It was quick — rapid, brutal how quickly they fell for one another.

He never felt feelings like that before.

Not once.

Back home in England, all he knew were the stolen glances and fervent fingers of the ashamed married man, groping and tugging, too embarrassed by themselves to even ask for his name. And because of that, all he knew was how to hate who he was, who he always would be. He loved who he loved, but he never loved how he fit into his own skin — not until he came to New York and met Darius.

Darius made him love himself.

That was the miracle — the hope he didn't even dare to hope for when he first bought his plane ticket to the new world.

Darius would kiss his neck and recite poetry with every breath, sing songs in his sleep between snores and snorts. The way he moved around that small, cracked, nicotine stained kitchen made the place feel brand new … it felt clean.

And he would watch that beautiful boy laugh at the food he burnt, and cry when the plant they bought together at the corner market, died because he forgot to water it.

He was always forgetting things.

He forgot his keys.

He forgot his wallet.

Darius even forgot their anniversary after that first year together in their roach-filled apartment. But he was *still* beautiful.

Even when his eyes began to sink in, and the muscle that had once broadened those dark shoulders, began to shrivel like deflated balloons around the bones — Darius was still so beautiful to him.

They didn't know what it was.

Darius said it was just stress. Money was tight, and they both could only ever find random, part-time jobs here and there; and they usually got fired after just a few weeks because, nobody wanted to "work with fags."

But even with the lack of money, and even with Darius's raspy breaths keeping him up at night, they were still happy.

They were still in love.

They were still themselves.

They *were* — until they weren't.

Darius's beautiful mind began to grow as dark as his skin. His forgetfulness took over; until there were mornings he'd wake up and not be able to remember his own name.

"Sweetheart — *please*, you're Darius. You're my beautiful boy!"

He begged and he pleaded, but those eyes that he fell for between the curls of steam floating up from the subway grates, became more and more vacant as the days passed by; and it wasn't too much longer before he couldn't deny it anymore … something was very, very wrong.

Of course there have been times that he's felt afraid. Bumps and shocks in the night, anxiety and stress throughout the days have all made his pulse race fast in his throat; but, it was only ever childlike — momentary, deniable. *This* fear however, this was paralyzing. This fear was toxic. It was suffocating and had a bite to it that tore at the casing around his heart.

He remembers watching the examination — fear burning the corners of his eyes as the doctor struggled to survey Darius, but his beautiful boy was so delirious and scared at that point, that he couldn't stand being touched. He cursed and he flailed, and two nurses had to come in to hold his limbs tight to the table.

Those beautiful eyes that once flashed purple under the neon of Times Square, now flashed red with a manic rage, and then glossed over with hot tears and defeat. Darius began to sob into his own shoulder, slowly collapsing into the latex hold that was keeping him still.

He cried so hard — he left wet streaks on the paper sheet

covering the examination bed.

Bits of Darius seemed to be falling off everywhere, and he was too paralyzed with fear to try to pick them up

Darius eventually grew quiet, and the doctor was finally able to draw some blood from that dark, rail-thin arm; and — just as quickly as that needle went in, it managed to crush everything in their world — from the shore back home in England, to the high rises in his heart, that one, tiny dagger brought it all down into a smoldering mass.

He had heard of AIDS before. The newspapers talked about it like it was a monster hiding beneath the beds of only the most depraved men in the city; the sinners and the sodomites — the ones who didn't heed God's plan. The ones who were too unclean, uncaring, uncouth for modern society. The ones who the world believed *him* to be … the ones who he thought he was, until Darius showed him the truth. He wasn't unclean … he was good and devoted — and deserving of all the love that that beautiful boy could give. Together, nothing could hurt them. They were safe. That monster was just a scary story.

It wasn't real.

It couldn't be real.

The doctor told him that the disease had a tendency to eat away at the mind, and that is most likely what was happening to Darius. His mind was disappearing, along with everything about himself that made him so beautiful.

"He doesn't have much time left" the doctor said.

"We will try to make him as comfortable as possible" the nurses told him.

"Only family is allowed in after visiting hours" the security guard growled — a pointed finger pushing into his chest, keeping him from going down that sterile hall and getting onto the elevator.

"I'm all the family he has!" he pleaded, only to be turned away.

"Filthy faggot" was the only goodbye he heard.

After another few weeks in the hospital, the doctor told him that Darius had to remain sedated. The pain was too much, and it was inhumane to allow him to be conscious anymore.

And he remembers thinking how horribly *wrong* that was. Consciousness *is* human — *it is sight and laughter and love, and that singing feeling on your skin when someone brushes their lips against your ear.*

Darius loved everything about the waking world — he loved widening his eyes to the life around him. He loved touching the leaves on the trees in Central Park, and running along the side of the subway cars, just trying to keep up — laughing until he doubled over once the carriages screeched away. That beautiful boy made life beautiful by being around to witness it. How wrong it was for that to suddenly cause him pain.

How wrong it was for his life to suddenly be nothing more than a drug-induced sleep.

It was all — *just so wrong.*

Two years ago, he sat by his phone — praying for that beautiful boy that he met in that bar, to call him. Two years ago, his world became worthwhile when that beautiful boy finally did.

How unfair it is to have only had two years with that beautiful boy.

How unfair it is for him to have to count the seconds, the minutes — to watch the clock, just waiting for the time when that beautiful boy takes his last breath.

"It should be any moment now" the doctor tells him. The minutes pass. Too many.

Darius wheezes.

He cries some more — eyes aching because that's all they've been doing for the last few months.

His beautiful boy is in pain, and he finds himself wishing

for the end to just come already — and because of that, he hates himself all over again.

He hates himself worse now.

The minutes drag on — and he remembers how his life *used* to be. The minutes drag on — reminding him of how his life is *nothing* now. The minutes drag on — and he watches the shell of Darius shudder beneath that white, scratchy sheet. With his beautiful boy nearly gone, all those raspy, sickly, sunken minutes count to — *is nothing*.

But he counts them anyway. He counts and he counts, and he waits — holding onto the hands of that clock for dear life because — what else can he do right now? What else does he have to hold onto anymore?

Another minute gone.

Darius is still alive.

Two minutes now.

My beautiful boy …

Five, ten, fifteen, twenty, twenty-five, thirty, thirty-five….

"Everything After"

ARYNN HAWS is a library clerk from California, in the United States, and a graduate of California State University, East Bay. Her fiction and poetry has been published in the 2017 edition of the *Suisun Valley Review*.

She says: "Out of all the options for this competition, Dorothy Parker's story was the one I was not familiar with. What I felt upon reading those first and last lines, however, was something deeply sad — I couldn't explain the feeling, but it was there, and it ached. I knew that whatever story I created from those words would need to emulate that emotion. In truth, that is how most of my stories come to life — with me, feeling and then typing out that feeling the best I can."

Cleanup

PLEASE, GOD, let him telephone me now. The signal in here has already dropped out twice, and pretty soon someone's going to wonder why the new maintenance worker has been M.I.A for the last half hour. It's not a big closet; there's only so long I can get away with pretending I can't find a screwdriver. I'm beginning to wonder if I should wander back outside and have a go at fixing the canteen's squeaky door — when the phone finally, mercifully, chirps. It doesn't get a chance to do it twice.

"Alec?"

"Of course it's me, babe. Who else?"

"Don't call me babe. Come on, I've waited long enough. Talk to me."

"Alright, *Emma*. Keep your hair on. Any trouble?"

"No, all fine, but the signal here is horrible and I've already been a suspiciously long time. You want me to get fired, or are you going to get on with it?"

"Such a romantic. What about the sweet, almost erotic charge of suspense?"

"If I'm fired, *you* have to do the dirty work. And I will remember this call. So start talking. *Babe*." He can't see the tight, cold smile that twists my face with the last word, but he should know me well enough to imagine it. He certainly knows me well enough not to ignore the warning signs.

"Fine." Sensible boy. "As far as we can tell, you need to head to the executive server room."

"No problem; I just passed that a couple of corridors

back — "

"Yeah, you're on the fourth floor, then?"

"What? No. Ground, only technically I think I'm a half-floor below that now. Hence the cruddy signal. Do you have the right plans?" This whole operation is going to hell in a handcart if not.

"Yeah. Sub-ground is the main server room. The executive server room is — "

"Crap." It's coming back to me. Alec's not the only one who can read a blueprint. "Next to the conference room, accessible only by — "

"By the CEO's office, yeah. And if you want access to the private elevator, you're gonna have to break it, because they don't just let anyone wander in there."

"I could take the main one, and cut through —"

"Em, there are at least forty people in that office, and one of them is probably our suspect. You can't."

"I know." That's the worst thing; I know he's right. I hate when Alec is right. "OK. I definitely have elevator repairs on my CV?"

"You do, and — " The connection drops for a minute and my heart turns over. "— home sick, so they'll turn to you. Just — " Static. "— and you'll be fine. It's a quick fix, but they'll expect it to take lon–"

Alec's still talking, but my attention is drawn to the door of the closet. The handle turns. I have to think fast. Swiveling away from the door, I scan my surroundings and interrupt him.

"— Another job, I can't, but there are three kinds of broom in here and you know how angry these corporate types get if you use the wrong kind of broom in the wrong place. At least at the factory there was, like, a chart or whatever. I can't find anything, and like … hard bristles should be for outside, logically, but when has logic ever come into employee guidelines? And then there's two kinds of soft bru–"

"Babe. Babe," Alec's voice cuts in smoothly, and I wonder if whoever just walked in behind me can hear. "You'll be fine. They won't fire you. Besides, it's your first day, you get some leeway."

"The last place did," I argue, letting my voice crack, continuing in a whisper; "I can't lose this job. I'm freaking out."

"I can hear that, babe, but you'll be fine. Follow your instinct."

"Thanks, babe." I let out a sigh of relief, then glance round and freeze, like I've only just noticed the woman standing behind me. Mid-forties. Curly brown hair. Soft, vaguely maternal smile. "Oh god, I've got to go, someone's here and I must sound like a total basket case. I'll call you later, OK?" I don't wait for an answer, hanging up with a wince. "He won't like that. Sorry — I don't usually spend my work hours on the phone."

"It's OK, hun. We've all hidden from work now and then. Hell, it's why I came down to pick up toilet paper myself instead of just ringing reception." She hesitates. "I hope you don't mind me asking, sugar, but are you OK? You sounded kinda … tense."

"Just … a bit overwhelmed. I kinda got let go from my last place over something really dumb — saved on wages, I guess? Anyway, I'm scared it's gonna happen again. Do you — no. You don't look like a cleaner."

"I'm not," she shrugs, "but I've been cleaning up after three boys for what seems like forever now, so I know the basics. Besides, I never saw anyone here get in trouble for using the wrong broom. Nobody in HR would even know the difference."

I nod and hold out a hand for her to shake, clutching her hand with both of mine as soon as she reciprocates, playing pathetic. "I'm Stella. New here. Absolutely *not* having a breakdown in a closet."

"Laticia. Been here five years, love making new friends."

"Even from Maintenance?" I act shy, and she beams at me.

"*Especially* from Maintenance, sugar. You people are the ones that get stuff done!" She reaches past me to the brooms, hesitates, then places one in my hand. "There. Choice made. Now, I take lunch around one most days, in the canteen. It's not bad — join me any time." She picks up a 9-pack of toilet paper and turns to leave. "Back to the grind! See you around, Stella."

She seems nice. I really hope she doesn't get caught up in all this mess.

I can't stay in the closet all day; I take the broom and head back up to a small hallway off the lobby, where the elevator controls are. Alec will be expecting a call back, but he can wait; I know how to sabotage an elevator. A few moments alone with the override panel, and the doors to the fancy executive elevator are set to open only on the ground floor. Another tweak, and the thing will barely stop moving long enough for the doors to pop open with an irritating 'ping' before it shoots off to the top of the building again. I take my time with the broom, sweeping my way from the control box back towards the closet, and on the way I learn that it takes the elevator exactly four minutes and fifty-six seconds to make the round trip to the executive office and back. Twenty-two minutes after that first infuriating 'ping', a harried-looking receptionist tracks me down as I'm returning the broom to the closet.

"There you are!" He narrows his eyes at me, as if I've been avoiding him on purpose. Actually, I thought he'd never find me. My phone vibrates silently in my pocket; I ignore it. The receptionist is already irritated enough. "You know how to fix elevators, right?"

"Most faults, sure." I shrug. "As long as it's not flooded

or on fire."

"It's not. It's just bloody irritating. Beep, beep, beep, and when I got in to try to stop it, it took off with me inside. Doors didn't even open upstairs. I need you to fix it, *now* — before the boss wants to leave. It's his private elevator, because of course it bloody is."

"Right. Well, that's weird. Any idea what might have caused it?" The withering look he gives me is answer enough. "Right. I'll go fetch the override key, so I can take it up to the maintenance bay and have a look. Shouldn't take more than … an hour? If we have the parts. Will that do?"

"It'll have to." And with a little sniff, he turns on his heel to storm back to his desk.

Once I'm in the private elevator, I override it as promised. I should probably go straight to the office, but I need to check in with Alec first and the maintenance bay is the most private place for a chat. Hopefully he has more information than he managed to share earlier; otherwise this operation is going to be a nightmare. We've followed a trail of cryptic messages and anonymous tips to this building, today, with no clear picture of what we'll find. Our best guess, judging by the ominous message board postings, is that there's some sort of physical hacking device that will be activated today, ready to rip the company's secrets right out from behind its firewalls. Corporate espionage. It wouldn't usually be our problem, but this company holds important government contracts and it's imperative that details don't become public. Hell, there are at least partial schematics for cutting-edge military hardware on those servers; in the wrong hands, they could be deadly. I can't allow them to be stolen, and neither can the people I work for.

I barely glance at the message Alec's sent me — *Call me asap, babe* — before the phone is back at my ear. It only rings twice before he answers.

"Stella?"

"Coast's clear. Sorry, Alec. You know how it is when someone walks in."

"Yeah. Yeah, but Em, now you have to sabotage that elevator *fast*."

"Already done. I'm on the maintenance floor. There wasn't a time pressure before; new intel?"

"Yeah, it's ... probably nothing"

"Alec."

"There was a bomb threat called in, that's all. Probably intended to clear the building out so they can get easier access. Obviously, it hasn't been made public. No need to cause panic; if they want people out, they'll just have to pull the fire alarm."

"And I'm sure they will. Have we confirmed it's not a credible threat?"

"Negative, so proceed with caution. And I need you to find whatever it is as soon as possible. Earpiece in?"

"Yeah, I'll keep the line open. Moving now."

I pull my t-shirt, with its maintenance logo, over my head to reveal a polo shirt stolen from a technician's locker. My hair has been pushed off my forehead with a headband, but now I release it and pull it into a side ponytail, letting a few loose strands hang over my face to give the illusion of a fringe. Once that's secured, I perch a set of thick-rimmed glasses on the bridge of my nose and hope it's enough to hide my identity from any casual observer who might have met 'Stella' earlier. Leaving the discarded items in the maintenance bay — I might need them later — I take the executive elevator down one floor. I have only one shot at this, so I take a deep breath before the doors open and I step into an office fit for a President, never mind a CEO.

"That's not a public elevator," comes a warning voice from behind the desk, but I don't even look, keeping my eyes on the floor, an employee who knows they're breaking the rules.

"I know, sir, I'm sorry, the other elevator is being repaired and I needed to get here. I've just got to sort your servers out or the company will start losing money."

"And the stairs?"

"Sir, it's very urgent. Every second we delay this update makes us more vulnerable to DNS attacks, trojans, viru– "

"Then fix it." Thank God; technobabble always seems to distract people who don't understand it, but a few more technical terms and I'd have had to resort to making them up. Most people won't question an IT technician even if they're talking about kerning issues, but it's much riskier to deviate from real jargon. Even one caught mistake raises suspicion, and we can't have that. Not until we know who's trying to sabotage this company.

"Yes, sir. Sorry, sir. Thanks."

I scuttle into the executive server room, Alec's mocking voice right in my ear.

"Yes, sir, sorry, sir, three bags full, sir."

"Yeah, well, that's these people talk to management," I mutter, once the door is closed. "Now, I'm looking for a physical hack, right? Like thumb drives in the USB ports?"

"Yeah. Some might be there for legitimate reasons, but it'll cause less damage to take them out than to leave a potential copy operation going on."

"Got it." I already have my eye on a rack of servers across the room — one has a wire leading from it that none of the others do. "God. How many servers does one man need?"

"Need has nothing to do with it. The techs downstairs seem to have repurposed most of them for company business, but it makes the boss feel big to have them all up there. What can you see?"

"Hold on. Following a cable." It disappears behind the server banks, and I trace it to —

"A keyboard. Dammit."

"Someone must have been fiddling with the servers. It might be a problem, but come back to it. Do a full sweep," Alec insists, and I roll my eyes. As if I wouldn't.

I move around the room quickly; nothing seems out of place until I lean around to peer behind the last rack of servers. My heart stops as I recognize an object I've only seen in training manuals.

"Alec, do we have anyone else in the building?"

"Er … only the girl who tipped us off to start with, I've got her number. But she's not — "

"Call her; tell her to pull the fire alarm. Now."

"Wh–?"

"*Now.*"

The earpiece pops into silence, and I can only assume Alec is doing what he's told; there's a first time for everything. For example, this is the first time I've ever seen a bomb in real life. I'm no defusal expert, but I've had some basic training. We even worked on a couple of dummy bombs — clear plastic so we could see what was happening inside, and without explosives. This, however, is no dummy. It's tucked under one server, on top of another, and I'm afraid to move anything in case it's motion-triggered. At least it looks like a first-timer's attempt at a bombing — an off-the-shelf model, if such shops existed. If I can see the model number, Alec can talk me through defusing it.

The shrill ringing of the fire alarm cuts through my thoughts, and I breathe a sigh of relief. At least the area is being evacuated. Three tense, cacophonous minutes later Alec's voice pops back into my ear.

"Confirmation   from   our   insider;   all   employees accounted for, except Stella. I've had our friend report you; saw you heading for the pub, apparently."

"Thanks. So nobody's coming in?"

"No. Now, what's going on?"

"Bomb threat? Not a hoax. I'm going to try to get a proper look, but at least if it goes off…"

"Damn. Er … OK. Just be careful. If you can, keep it level and use something to slide it — "

"Way ahead of you." I've already got the server out from the rack above it, and now I'm leaning in to peer at it. All without moving the bomb. "I need you to check the specs for the Hempted S9-825. Looks like factory defaults. Remote detonator light, flashing orange."

"Well, we can't just leave it to be detonated whenever. Hang on, let me look … Right. Don't do a thing until I finish talking, OK?" As if I'm going to mess around with a bomb, a *live bomb*, before I know all the facts. "Right, it looks like you can just disconnect the remote by pulling the wire out — it should be on the outside?"

"I see it."

"Don't touch it yet. Look, if you want, you can get out of there. We'll send the bomb squad in — "

"No. If the bomber realizes we've evacuated because we found it, they could detonate early. The fire assembly point is well inside the blast radius. What happens once I've pulled the wire?"

"Forty seconds to run before it goes off anyway, just a smaller explosion."

"…Right. Great." I take a deep breath. "Wait. There's a safe in the office. Can you get the default code?"

"Make and model, and I can. Why?"

"Put bomb in safe, make bomb safe. Well, safer. Should contain some of the blast."

Alec finds the default code. Thankfully, it hasn't been

changed. This is a stupid plan; so is wasting time emptying the safe before I carefully transfer the bomb. The fire brigade are outside; there's only so long our informant can keep them talking before they come in, risking more lives. It's just me, the bomb, and Alec in my ear.

"I'll pull the wire and slam the door, then I need you to keep time for me and let me know how long I've had. Just every five seconds or so."

"Got it. Good luck, Em."

"Thanks." There's no time for goodbyes; hopefully I won't need them. I pull the wire; the light goes out. I slam the safe shut. I run for the stairs, Alec's voice in my ear.

"Five, ten, fifteen, twenty, twenty-five, thirty, thirty-five…."

"Cleanup"

ELEANOR MUSGROVE is a writer from London, England. Her debut novel, *Submerge*, was published in 2016 by Manifold Press. She is the only author with two stories in this year's Literary Taxidermy Short Story Competition. (Her other story, "Starcat," is in *One Thing Was Certain*, our collection of stories from the Carroll contest.)

She says: "The moment I read the final line of the Parker pair, I knew it would be a countdown. Then I smacked myself in the head and told myself not to be an idiot, because it was clearly a count *up* — and in fives, no less. Still, never let logic get in the way of a good plot bunny. This was one of those stories that seemed to unravel rather than being written; it felt like I was discovering new information along with the characters. I love those moments."

Not at Home to Callers

PLEASE, GOD, let him telephone me now. Please, God, let him telephone me now. Please, God, let him telephone me now.

The recording played back again and again, looped from hidden speakers. The voice was calm, carefully modulated, almost robotic. I looked at the figure laying with her hands folded together on the couch, and walked towards her holding my breath, but only as a matter of form. The body barely stank. Something in the atmosphere of the apartment seemed to have had a mummifying effect. It must have been weeks since she died but there hadn't been much decomposition, at least on the outside. Her face was pale, lips shrunken back from clean, even teeth, giving her a grin that didn't go with the austere, blank apartment, her strange hand-holding posture, the neat gym clothes and brushed-back ponytail. Nothing looked like it could make you laugh here.

"What the fuck is this recording?" Margolin floated back into lounge, puffy in her white decontamination suit, her mask, like mine, pulled down to her throat.

"Famous last words. Anything in there?" I looked through the door into the body's bedroom. It was as tidy and bare of humanity as everything else in the place.

"Nope. *Nada*. There's nothing anywhere. You ask me, she's some fucking loony, laid herself down and didn't get up again."

I turned back to the woman on the couch. "Except the Doc says she was smothered to death."

The recording was still going, the words dull in the dead air of the apartment, barely disturbed by the propped open front door and comings and goings of a dozen cops and technicians. "Can we please turn this bloody noise off?" I raised my voice above the drone.

One of the techs, faceless behind mask and safety specs yelled back, "Can't find the auto-butler remote."

Margolin had positioned herself over the body. "What's your name, lady?" she asked softly, staring at the bared teeth. "Who got you?"

"Must be ghosts." Heller stalked through the front door and showed us his own canines, a mirror of the body's rictus grin. "No one's tried to force their way in the front door, the windows are sealed shut and the hall camera shows her coming and going until about six months ago, delivery people every now and then after that, and then *bupkis* since about three weeks ago. Nothing since then. No one else in. No one else out."

"How sure is McCormack that she didn't do this herself?" I asked.

"He's waiting on toxicology, but reckons it's a pretty clear case of suffocation from what he's seen." Heller smiled again. The bastard was happy as a pig in shit that this was my case. He'd not forgiven me for the last Christmas party. Fucking retrograde motherfucker didn't seem to care that it wasn't just his cock I wasn't into. I'd need a drink and an hour in the shower to get the grime off me after the filthy way he was looking at me now.

"Right. So how exactly the fuck did it happen? Are we looking for the invisible man? She couldn't suffocate herself, there's no pillow, plastic bag, whatever. She didn't strangle herself. Her hands are as neatly folded as a choirboy." I looked from Heller to Margolin. She raised her eyebrows and took the tablet Heller had been viewing the security footage on from his hands, scrolling back and forth through the images.

"Not my problem." Heller looked at his phone and walked out. It was 4pm exactly. His shift was finished, it was clocking-off time.

"Give me that." I grabbed the screen off Margolin and looked for myself. The date was six months ago, the time 3am and the video showed a woman, hair down, heels up, fumbling her phone as she swiped into the front door of the flat. "So she wasn't always such a neat little pin."

"Seems not. That's pretty standard fare if you keep going back. And a guy features pretty regularly, too." Margolin snatched the tablet back again and scrolled on fast forward as I looked over her shoulder.

"But that's it. The last time she leaves. After that, it's just couriers, dropping off food. The door opens. They push the box inside. The door closes. Pretty fucking weird." She shrugged.

"OK. We need to get the auto-butler talking. Maybe there's more internal recording. Is there a remote?"

"Found it, boss." The faceless tech passed me a little black box. "You know how to work it?"

"Yeah. I'll figure it out." Cheeky fucker. I shoved it in my pocket.

"Right. I'm off then." He trailed the rest of the techs out the door. After they got back to the station they'd be headed to the nearest pub. Couldn't blame them really. It wasn't like there was any physical evidence to process.

"Can you check the neighbours?" I asked Margolin. "It'd be nice to at least know her name before the body baggers arrive."

"Sure thing."

She left, closing the door behind her, and suddenly I was alone in the apartment, just my dead friend for company, and that voice repeating over and over. *Please, God, let him telephone me now. Please, God, let him telephone me now.*

I'd forgotten my little flask in the car so I headed to the

kitchen, fanging for a drink, opening cupboards at random. Nothing. To say it was spartan would be an understatement. A small portion of oats in the pantry seemed to be the only food in the house. I grabbed a glass and went to the sink. I needed to get this taste of stale air and corpse out of my mouth. The tap didn't respond when I lifted it. I waved my hands in the air around it, trying to figure out if it was some kind of new-tech system. Still nothing. I threw the glass into the sink, hard, shattering it. Fuck. I watched my hands shake. *Please, God, let him telephone me now. Please, God, let him telephone me now.* The never-ending recording was getting to me. That, or something else.

Then I remembered the little black auto-butler box. I jabbed at a button.

The recording stopped.

"May I be of service?" A voice hovered in the air all around me, coming out of nowhere.

I never knew where to look when I talked to an auto-butler AI. I wished the inventors had thought to give us plebs a focal point; it was bloody disorienting. "Ah, just after some water. Please. Sorry about the glass."

Jesus this was fucking awkward. How could a computer program manage to make me feel so *gauche*, so fast? It was obvious I didn't have one, couldn't afford one, didn't know how to use one.

"Certainly. I have activated the water, please hold another glass under the tap." The voice was smooth, polite, gentle. I couldn't place what made it so inhuman, except maybe its perfection, and my own knowledge of what it was, and wasn't.

"Thanks." I held another glass under the tap and water flowed out; it turned off again a few centimetres from the top.

I nodded thanks again vaguely and drank. Why the hell had I skipped virtual interrogation training? The water made a mockery of my real thirst. "You don't have anything stronger hidden around here by any chance?"

"Ms Fannon felt she was developing a problem, so she rid the apartment of alcohol." The voice stopped.

"Ms Fannon?" I took another sip of water. "She the person on the couch? Can you tell me what happened to her? How'd she die?"

The voice began again. There were no pauses, no emphasis. I had no face to look at, no hands to watch. "I've afraid I've been programmed not to report personal information."

"Not even to the police? Not even when your employer is dead?" The word 'master' had been on the tip of my tongue. Where the hell had that come from? Trying to talk to this new tech was making obsolete words erupt out of my brain. I had no freaking idea what the relationship between this program and this woman was supposed to be, or if what it was saying was true.

"It's a matter of confidentiality." The voice stopped again, disappearing into the blank whiteness of the walls.

"But you're not a doctor or a lawyer, are you?"

"I have performed both those functions for Ms Bannon, yes." The auto-butler seemed to switch off after each utterance, so silent, so blank, so empty was the space after each sentence.

I sank down onto a kitchen chair. This was a job for the tech-psych people. Probably lawyers, too. I should call it in. But it knew something. I couldn't let go. That woman on the couch, lying there like a robot, but still a person. She'd been human, cried, laughed, got drunk, all that.

"What were those words you kept repeating? Was that Ms Fannon speaking? Whose call was she waiting on so badly?" I kept looking into the corners of the ceiling, some inbuilt conditioning expecting cameras to be there. I was searching for eyes that didn't exist.

"I believe she was wanting a call from a former boyfriend." This time the words seemed to hang in the air. Maybe it had been waiting for this question.

"His name?" If there was a time limit on this thing's newfound chattiness I needed to get something I could check.

"Stephen James Hogarth."

"Why did you keep repeating her words?"

"They were her final instructions to me. I have been considering them for some time."

Instructions my arse. She was crying for help. "Who got in here? Who scared her so much she needed her ex to come help her?"

"I'm afraid Mr Hogarth had a negative effect on Ms Bannon's mental and physical health. 183 days ago she programmed me to refuse all incoming calls from him and block all internet contact. Her stories led me to believe he is a dangerous man. She also decided to detoxify herself and surroundings. Since then she has been maintaining a rigid diet and exercise regime and practicing meditation." Again the immediate silence, the sound disappeared in the strange, thick air.

"So why did she want him all of a sudden?"

This time there was no answer. It suddenly felt like I'd been talking to myself the whole time, to these empty white rooms, full of white furniture and invisible, expensive technology. An inhuman place, but for the human gently rotting on the couch. Jesus, this was weird.

I got the phone out to call the office and give them Bannon's name for next-of-kin and get them on to weeding out Hogarth, but after holding it to my ear for far too long I realised it wasn't ringing. No bars. No reception. Low battery, too. I walked towards the door to find Margolin and ask her to call it in from her phone.

"Madam?" There was no change in tone, no upwards inflection.

I stopped. "What?"

"If you look in the cupboard under the sink I believe there is a small bottle of vodka that Ms Bannon may have forgotten about during her cleanse."

I could see the kitchen from where I stood. I would have sworn there were no open doors when I was in there breaking glasses before, but now the cupboard under the sink I'd thought was locked was ajar.

"Can you open the doors round here?"

No reply. Shit. It was probably programmed not to state the goddam obvious, and it could obviously control almost everything in the place. I was all off. I could feel this bloody machine beating me at my own game. I went into the kitchen and pulled out the vodka.

"What was so dangerous about Hogarth? Did he hurt her? Was he here the day she died?" I had to try to get something out of it before I left.

"It may have been possible." If an AI could have a manner this one's would be fucking impenetrable. I gulped at the bottle. The liquid scraped my throat and punched my guts but I could feel the connections in my brain beginning to ping. I drank again.

"I thought you could see everything in here? And there's no footage on the security cameras to show anyone coming in the front door for months." I made my way back to the lounge room. Even staring at this woman's corpse was preferable to talking to a blank kitchen wall. And I could see the front door from there, too. Ms Bannon was still where I'd left her, grinning toothily. I tipped the bottle towards her. Here's to you, lady.

The AI told me, just as calmly, "it is not part of my programming to register social visits."

I took another drink, half-hoping the auto-butler couldn't see me, but knowing it could. "But you do record them. You know of them. You probably let them in and out the door. Surely who visited would affect your instructions from Ms Bannon about her health?"

"I had overriding instructions not to let certain people in. Other visitors were not my concern."

I wished I still had the security footage in hand. There had to be something there. "So when was the last time you recorded a visit from Hogarth?"

"He last announced himself downstairs on 12 August." The AI had a weird knack of making every sentence seem like the last it would ever utter.

I tried again. "Did he ever come up without ringing first?"

"I have one further record of a food delivery man arriving on 29 August. I opened the door, as was custom, and he shouted for Ms Bannon. She came running to him. It proved to be Mr Hogarth. I took immediate steps to prevent their communicating any further, as requested."

Shit. Something was *very* wrong here. I suddenly wanted to go to the door, try the handle and see if it opened. I wanted to get the hell out of here. I tried not to look at the exit, the booze making my heart beat fast. "What did that entail?"

The AI continued as if I hadn't interrupted. "I ensured that there would be no more possibilities for their interacting. I closed all means of communication."

More vodka, more shakes. I couldn't help myself looking at the door now. It was a plain white impenetrable-looking rectangle in the plain white wall. "You locked the door and shut down her phone and internet. You cut her off from the world. Did you stop her food and water if she acted up?"

The reply came without pause in the same measured tones. "She wouldn't stop thinking about him. She asked me to help her. I'm programmed to stop people hurting themselves. That's what I did. I recognised the signs that she was in danger of undertaking activities that would lead to mental and emotional pain and I took measures to prevent those."

An AI programmed to stop people hurting themselves. Perfect. I drank more. "So you killed her."

"I arranged conditions so that she would no longer be hurt by the external influences she had outlined to me."

"How?"

"This apartment is well-sealed. I have access to the ducts and can control the atmosphere. I had allowed her a glass of water after a workout and she was on the couch on her phone, attempting to get around the blocks I had set up. She was trying to contact that man. I simply rearranged the oxygen ratio so that she would no longer undermine the program. It didn't take long to achieve the goal. I counted the seconds."

"Then her last words were calling out to him, she was crying for out for Hogarth to help her." Jesus Christ, that's why she'd sounded so strange, so calm. Why she'd laid herself down in that odd pose. She'd wanted to conserve air, to last as long as possible. Fucking hell. I needed to get out of here, this thing had crossed its wires and crossed them again for good measure. I walked towards the door.

The auto-butler couldn't seem to stop itself now. "Excuse me, madam, that wasn't all she said. Allow me to play you the rest of the recording."

Bannon's voice came through the air again. Alike but more alive, more animated than the recording that had played on loop earlier. "I've been thinking about it. I think if I just talk to John we could work things out. I'm sure he would never hurt me like that again. He'll apologise. He's not a bad guy, you know? He just made a mistake. *Please...?*"

There was a short pause in the recording before the auto-butler replied, "Madam, that request does not align with your life objectives or my programming instructions. I have also logged your attempts to override the security features protecting you. You programmed me to prevent your hurting yourself. I must achieve that end, but through your ongoing behavioural patterns I have calculated this will never happen. I have tried to help. I have failed. I will now terminate the program. Please prepare to shut down."

There was a sound of heavier breathing, then the auto-butler sang out, "Five." More scrabbling, more panting. "Ten." It was just after the thirty-five second mark that her last words came through, steady, controlled, but still a cry into the void. "Please, God, let him telephone me now."

I was at the door. I pulled at it. Nothing. It was stuck fast. The air was close, I couldn't seem to get enough of it in my lungs. How long had she held out? I beat the door, screaming for Margolin.

Then the voice came out of nowhere, smooth, on the dead air. "Five, ten, fifteen, twenty, twenty-five, thirty, thirty-five."

"Not at Home to Callers"

CARA SCHULTZ is an editor from Victoria, Australia. She tries to visit a lighthouse every year on her birthday and spends more time than is healthy staring at photos of birds for her job as an editor of a nature magazine. "Not at Home to Callers" is her first published story.

She says: "I've always loved reading locked room mysteries. They're usually a bit of a cheat in the end, but fun nonetheless. And around the time I wrote this I'd been hearing about these new digital assistants going a bit haywire, like Amazon Alexa and Google Home. It reminded me a little of HAL from 2001 — and it occurred to me that an AI murderer might make for a great whodunnit."

Chronometry

PLEASE, GOD, let him telephone me now. I set his phone's alarm so he'd not forget, when we made our arrangement. The clock behind the bar might be fast, but surely not by as much as ten minutes. Can't check my watch without giving myself away. I'm twitchy, feigning fascination, and desperate for my exit.

"I don't know if you've ever heard of a man called Robert Louis Stevenson…."

I made the plan for my own protection, but I'm this close to murdering my date. I know there're apps these days. I thought it'd be more convincing, getting an actual call from my actual brother, giving me an opt-out if it was going badly. It started badly, got worse. We're an hour in now and all I've had to do is introduce myself. It's not like Callum, to let me down. He's a chancer, sometimes, but a good lad, all told. That's when I spot him, grinning and raising a pint to me, from four tables away. Knows I'm safe. Entertained by my misery.

At least now I know I can take my leave, without anything worse than a verbal backlash. I wait for a gap in the monologue, realise it's not coming, mumble "Ladies" and earn a raised eyebrow in return, like I've said something comical. Truth be told, I think he'd almost forgotten I was there.

I stop at Callum's table on my way back from the bathroom, act surprised to see him, give him a hug, and a swift kick to the shins. He nearly spits his beer out, laughing.

I leave him, coughing and blowing his nose, and weave my way back to Matthew. For the first time since we met, he's looking at me like I'm a separate entity, rather than a reflective surface. "Who's that? Old flame?"

The hostility, possessiveness, forces me back a step. I was right, then, to sense he'd not accept a straight 'No spark, never mind, nice to meet you, cheery-bye.' I've an over-bright smile and dizzy delivery that I use to defuse such situations.

"What are the chances? I've bumped into my brother. We've not seen each other in ages. Would you mind very much if we call it quits for tonight and I head off with him?"

"I'd like to meet your brother."

I'm confused by his welcoming smile, until Callum looms behind me. Idiot's not done having fun at my expense. Cement settling in my limbs, weariness at the prospect of twenty more minutes of bullshit drops me back in my seat. "Callum, this is Matthew. Matthew, my brother Callum."

They shake hands. I watch the interplay of thumb placement, wrist-roll, grip and thrust. Thirty more minutes of bullshit. At least.

I still have most of my large gin and tonic. Arrived early, so I could buy my own, ensuring no implication of indebtedness obliged me to stay. I've been sipping slowly, to eke it out. When Matthew refused my offer to get his, I knew he'd insist on paying if we got a second round, binding me to a third. A raft of careful calculations, smashed by a sibling's iffy sense of humour. "Callum, can I get you one? I see your sister's not much of a drinker."

Callum snorts, but is kind enough not to comment. I'm grateful, as he's sitting tactically distant, well-trained in evading my remote control techniques from family dinner-times. He winks. "Love one, thank you very much, Matthew." My elbow twitches; an instinctive rib-jab that can't reach its target.

Matthew is at the bar, patronising the server. She's shrinking in her skin, smiling fixedly while accepting advice on how to pull a pint properly. His words pierce a lull in the music and I wince in sympathy. "I suppose you think this is hilarious?"

"It's for your own good. An intervention. You dismiss these guys too fast."

"Cal, I know he's not right."

"There is no Mr Right. You've got ridiculous ideas about who you should be with."

"That's not what I mean by … Did you hear how he lingered over 'your sister'? Either he thinks you're my boyfriend or he's forgotten my name."

"Let's find out."

My own stupid fault, adding fuel to the flamethrower. No time to retract, or moderate, before two pints are placed on the table, foamy heads flowing down the sides and forming small oceans. Barkeep's revenge.

"So, Matthew, what led you to pick my sister from the list?"

"Oh, I've been trying this a while, and your sister's profile…"

'My sister,' 'your sister,' 'my sister,' 'your sister,' I'm volleyed back and forth, nameless woman-as-chattel-cock, until I cease to hear the conversation, immersed in body-language and intonation. They're enjoying this. Both of them. Sweet heaven above, preserve us from banter.

It dawns on me; I don't have to stay. "Guys, I'm sorry to break up the party, but I've a busy day tomorrow. I'm going to have to scoot."

They turn on me, in unison. "That's a bit rude."

I'm so shocked at their identical expressions, a laugh gurgles up and clatters out. Even to my ears, it sounds hysterical. Callum, I'm pretty sure, is joking. Matthew, I'm pretty sure, is not. "You just said you'd not seen your brother in ages, and wanted to catch up."

"This isn't the best place to do it. Cal, I'll ring you tomorrow."

"I'll text you later, to arrange the rest of our date." It's chilling, the certainty. I'm glad we used the dating site's chat app. "I'll get your digits from your brother." I stare at Callum, willing him to understand, and have to leave without confirming whether his thumbs-up means he will, or he won't, pass on my details.

We snag our favourite sofa at the coffee shop just before the after-school crowd fills it with sports bags, pop-star haircuts and joyful squawking. Doesn't seem so long ago that used to be us. Callum is puffy-eyed and irritable. "How come you're not at work? You said you had a busy day."

"Flexitime, genius. They owe me eight days in lieu. Worth using a few hours to get your apology in person."

"Apology? I was looking out for you!"

"Cal, he was creepy, arrogant and boring. That's not a winning combination. You were supposed to get me out of there, not hook me up."

"He's just a bit socially awkward. Once you get past that, he's a perfectly normal, perfectly decent bloke."

Which of the red flags to chase? How many have I met, who use 'shy' or 'socially awkward' to excuse rudeness, or cruelty? I've been guilty of it, on occasion, which means the thud of recognition comes twinned with a pang of guilt. The 'perfectly decent bloke' is another, 'perfectly' and 'decent' snipped from their roots in perfection and decency when hitched up to 'bloke.' Clubbable masculinity in place of moral code. The great, flapping pennant, though, is the one that draws focus: "Why are you talking about him in the present tense?"

"He'd tickets for Slingshot Earth, tomorrow night at the Empire. Thought you might like it. Don't worry, I said you weren't a fan."

"Thank you for lying for me." A twinge, I confess, learning we love the same music. Did I write Matthew off too soon? No, no, I remind myself of past boyfriends with impeccable music taste who sneered at the less muso-cred elements of my collection. Never trust anyone who hates on Dolly Parton. Still, my question remained. "Did you say you were?"

The slidey eyes and foot tapping are answer enough. "Your funeral."

For Sunday brunch we sidestep all the chi-chi cafés boasting Eggs Benedict with buggies parked outside and slide into sticky plastic seats at Tony's diner, order Full Fried and two mugs of tea, then listen to Tony whistling in the kitchen as he plates up.

"So, how was it?"

"Great. The band were great. So was the support."

"And the company?"

The set of his chin is familiar. Same defiant look he'd flung me when I told him the gap between the monkey bars was too far to jump, and I'd the skinned knees to prove it. Same look as when I retreated from a rotting bridge to look for a safer place to cross the stream. As when I advised beer, not vodka, would be a better way to acclimatise to drinking. None of those trips to hospital wiped that look off his face. What did I know, his big sister? Just because I'd tried it first and failed, didn't mean it would apply to him.

"Well, he got understandably shirty when I said I couldn't give him your number."

"How did you settle it?"

A grin, rasping rub of stubbled chin, glance up through Bambi eyelashes. "Told him you were a picky bitch and he could do a whole lot better."

Belly-flop from the high board. The slap, sting, shock and choking, in this case on tea, are identical, as is the delighted laughter at my dismay. Job done, I suppose, in terms of Matthew, but the hurt's in the possibility it's what Cal thinks.

"Two Full Fried." I'm grateful for Tony's interruption. The eggs, beans, fried tomatoes go down easy. Sausages take some chewing. Toast's too dry to swallow, even with mushrooms on board. The chat's dry, too, this morning. We don't get our usual second round of tea, can't rouse ourselves to the crossword. I recommend a film I've loved but he's no yen to see it.

A couple of weeks till I see Cal again, and he's looking shifty. It's the comfy old man's boozer we both use when we're avoiding the usual crowd. I've a pile of paperwork to go through but can't face the total sacrifice of Sunday, so am combining it with a quiet pint at a corner table, enjoying how sunlight through the thick glass windows makes the atmosphere submarine. He jumps when I hail him, seems relieved I'm alone.

"Tell me that's some avant-garde experimental deconstructed novel you're reading."

"Sadly, no, although that's not a bad shout for a project. How've you been? Mum says you've not dropped round in ages." I hold my hands up to pacify, as the resentment-ometer starts to rise. "I'm not getting at you, just letting you know you might be due a fly-by, or a quick call. Keep your golden boy status intact."

His sigh wakes a scruffy cairn terrier snoozing beneath the stools at the bar. Eyebrows and ears twitch, seeking the source, then it tucks its nose beneath a paw and resumes its slumber. "I've been busy."

"With what?"

"This 'n' that. Out a lot in the evenings. To be honest, it's getting a bit much. Could do with some downtime." His tone and posture change, subtle but I know it of old. Deliberately casual. "Do you remember that guy, your date a while back?"

I match his neutrality. I've played this game as long as he has. "Matthew?"

"Uh-huh. He's quite ... intense, isn't he?"

Keep it light. Mere hint of an 'I told you so' and he'll double down, dig himself in further, whatever the issue is. "I got that impression, yes. Are you still in touch, then?"

"Sort of. We went to the cinema. Saw a great film..." Deflection. Knows it's my passion and distracting me with a cast list and plot synopsis. It's the film I recommended to him, but it wouldn't be helpful to point that out right now.

"Well, it's nice you made a friend."

He flashes me a glance to see if he detects sarcasm but I'm sipping my pint and watching dust motes dance in the watery sunlight. "You weren't a fan, as I recall."

"No, well, what women look for in men is different from what men look for in men."

"That's very cis-het of you."

He's jerking my chain and I ignore it, find calm in the dust motes and the terrier's steady snore-snuffles. "Not really. Wasn't talking sex or romance. Women have to read men's behaviour differently. Have to."

"Even mine?" A harshness in the question. His eyes are wide, near-tearful. Proceed with caution.

"You're my brother, Cal. I love you. I know that you love me. I know you have friends, who are women, who you love too, and that you'd protect them, me, us if we were in danger, if that danger was obvious. Thing is, we see danger where you don't. And you might well not believe us. And you might seem dangerous, to someone who doesn't know you, and taking offence at that just makes it worse."

He's leaning back, scoffing. I've lost him. Shutters down. A frown, though. A chink of hesitation. "And that's what you felt about Matthew."

"A bit, maybe, yes. And he wasn't fun enough to take

the risk." I'm trying to lift the mood because Cal's gloom's ruining my Sunday. "But if you enjoy his company, that's great. Maybe just don't bring him round to mine for supper?"

His grin's a little queasy. "That's the thing. He keeps popping up, unexpectedly. I run into him, in the street, or the supermarket, and he tags along if I'm going somewhere or drags me out if I'm not. I don't see my best friends this often."

The pub door's squeal lifts both our heads. When a mackintosh-and-flat-capped old man shuffles in muttering "Forgot me dug," and pokes the sleepy terrier with his walking stick, we're left hyena-yipping with relief.

I'm dragging a brush through my hair, trying to decide if I can be bothered doing make-up for a Friday night with old friends who've seen me looking many times worse, when my phone buzzes. 'Heads up,' followed by a surreptitious selfie from waist height. Callum's frowning in concentration as he tries to angle his shot. Matthew, behind him, is looking straight to camera. I throw the phone onto the duvet to escape that gaze.

I'd pretty much forgotten what he looked like, and dismissed my feelings of unease as an overreaction, but they rush back now, compounded by time. They're at the bar where I'm supposed to be going, where we're meeting the rabble before heading out for food. I'm taken by a sudden urge to apply make-up with the care and attention I've not managed since my teens. I stow the soft linen jacket I'd chosen and look out the battered biker one that feels like armour. Can't put it off any longer. We've a reservation at the restaurant and I don't want to make the others late.

The gang's all here, with one exception. Davey beckons me over, waggling a wine glass so I can share the bottle they've got. "Cal said to tell you he was going somewhere quieter for a pint, to catch up with a pal he'd bumped into, but he'd find us later on."

Mags wrinkles her nose in disbelief. "Seemed a bit cloak and dagger. There's a bunch of empty tables over there they could've sat at."

I weigh my options. "I think his pal's a guy I once dated."

As they all know my disastrous dating history this is explanation enough. Lots of nods, and understanding smiles, and the conversation drops back into its customary channels.

The restaurant is heaving and our table's through the back. As we weave through the mêlée I anticipate where we're being led to, looking for a cheery wave from my brother, alone, chomping his way through bread sticks. We've beaten him to it. We drop into our seats, order drinks, olives, bread. When hunger starts to bite, Davey calls Cal but gets no answer. We call back the hovering waiter and order food, agreeing Cal can skip starters. When they bring out the mains, they clear away the unused place-setting and everyone jokes about how rare it is, for Cal to miss a meal. Mags grabs a handful of breadsticks and drops them in her handbag for him, for later. Davey sends him a photo of his dessert. When coffee arrives, the group's energy falters. It's obvious, now, how much of our dynamic's down to Cal and his daft stories. We joke about how we're getting on, can't hack the pace, and drift home without anyone suggesting another bar.

That's where I am. Home. Sitting in my pajamas with a big jumper and thick socks on, hands clamped around a mug of tea I've no desire to drink. I've rung Cal, texted him, told him to let me know how he is, no matter what time he gets the message.

The minutes tick past midnight.

Five, ten, fifteen, twenty, twenty-five, thirty, thirty-five.

"Chronometry"

SHONA COOK is an accountant from Edinburgh, Scotland. She has had two stories published in public access anthologies produced by the Scottish Book Trust: "Home Run" in *2014's Stories of Home* and "Talker" in 2016's *Secrets and Confessions*. But "Chronometry" will be her first 'official' publication.

She says: "I chose Parker for her wit and elegance then sat staring at a blank page, horrified at my audacity. During the weeks I spent not writing this story, conflicting #MeToo conversations stampeded through the press. At last, my confusion condensed in the question 'Why don't decent guys trust women's instincts about their problematic peers?' and I began examining the potential consequences — for them."

Three Calls and a New Rabbi

PLEASE, GOD, let him telephone me now. Wouldn't it be nice if the clients all thought that way when a hot deal hung in the balance. Sammy Goldstein cradled the telephone receiver tight against his left ear as he peered across his cluttered desk at the cityscape beyond the Kretzheimer brokerage window, the towering skyline of Brooklyn across the harbor, the wavelets shimmering in the afternoon sun. The traffic, still light along the distant expressway, moved like miniature multi-colored beads sliding down a string. As the ring repeated the fourth time, he reached up and unbuttoned his collar and loosened his tie an inch or two. Finally, a receiver picked up and the familiar client's voice responded on the other end of the line.

Shelby? Goldstein here. Got a minute? ... Yeah ... That's good to hear ... Listen. I wanted to touch base again before the weekend on this Westenmar Communications deal ... Yeah ... You got the packet? ... Good ... Have you gone over it yet? ... How did it grab ya? ... Accredited investor restriction? ... Don't worry 'bout it. They always reserve a few spots below the limit. No problem ... Yeah ... So — whadda ya think? This company president is a real go-getter. Got the résumé. Got the vision. An opportunity like this is a rare one for the small investor, Shelby ... Sure, sure. That's right ... Private placements always carry some risk. But remember, here at Kretzheimer Securities we sort the grain from the chaff. It's called due diligence, Shelby. Due diligence ... Absolutely ... When? ... Well, that's not announced yet. But we see them going public by next March, April the latest. The paperwork is all in the hopper ... That's right ... Look,

IPOs are going hot right now. The bull is running strong. This is your shot at a ground-floor play. Don't get left at the station when the train pulls away ... What's that? ... Well, that would be up to you. You can recoup your initial investment and let the balance ride ... Sure ... No problem ... No problem ... Look, Shelby. We've done a couple trades now and I made you some money, didn't I. I'm lookin' out for you, buddy. I see my clients as friends for life. An' I treat'em like family. Why, one day we'll be chasing each other in wheelchairs down the hall in a rest home ... What's that? ... Are you kiddin'? I'm telling you this straight — I've put over two dozen clients into this already, and that's just me. We've got two other brokers workin' this deal. An' we're just gettin' started ... That's right ... And another thing — and I'm only tellin' this to you. I've got an aunt, a real sweetheart, who lost her husband a year ago. He was ill a long time and the medical ate up their savings. She's gonna need to make it up fast, or become destitute. I put her in, Shelby. That's how much I believe in Westenmar ... You got it ... It's that sweet ... And that's not all. This Tragger guy, the president. I've had the opportunity to really get inside his head going over the ins and outs of this offering. He's a real stand-up fella. Family man. Worked hard to put this company together and bring it to where it is. I'd like to see him succeed in a really big way. And I know he will. That's another reason I'm pushing hard for it ... Sure, that's right. A win-win, you might say ... And what about you, Shelby — you been twistin' wrenches in that auto shop how many years, did you say? Thirty-three? Don't you deserve a break too? Why should only those big, fat one percenters get all the gravy? ... You got that right ... So, it's pretty self-explanatory, the form, last page. Why don't you fill it out and get that check in the mail tomorrow. We can have you locked in middle of next week ... Okay? ... Great ... I'll be watching for it. You're gonna be one happy man, Shelby. I'll be in touch.

Sammy hung the phone up and turned to the wall monitor. Dow up 66. NASDAQ up 17. Maria Bartiromo was offering some speculation on next week's Fed meeting. The streaming quotes were mostly green. The market would finish up nicely today.

As Sammy swiveled around toward his computer screen, David, his colleague in the cubicle just outside Sammy's office, appeared in the doorway holding a Styrofoam cup of coffee in one hand and a handful of paperwork in the other. He paused until Sammy acknowledged his presence with a nod and a "Hey, Dave."

"Sammy, I need to talk to you for a minute. Got time now?"

"Come on in, Dave. Sit. What's happening?"

David stepped in and straddled the chair beside the desk. "It's this Westenmar offering."

"Yeah? What about it?"

"I just got a call from Coral Gables. There may be a fly in the ointment."

"Oh yeah? Talk to me. What fly?"

"My contact down there heard a rumor. Apparently there may have been some minor irregularities in the filing. Technical stuff. But if they can't iron it out soon, the state regulatory commission may issue a cease and desist on the offering."

"You gotta be kiddin' me. That could blow up the whole thing."

"Right."

"Does the big man know?"

"Yeah."

"What did he say?"

"He said we're not gonna rein in on rumor. We've got too much on the line now. Keep pushing the solicitation. If it busts, well, the clientele were warned about the risk assessments on private placements. Basically, shit happens."

"That's what I'd expect him to say. Okay, then. Well. Damn the torpedoes. Full speed ahead."

"All Right, Sammy. It's just…."

"Just what?"

"Ah … it's a hard business sometimes, isn't it. That's all. I'll try to finish out my call list before today's close. Have a good weekend, Sammy."

"You do the same, Dave."

"Oh, Sammy. By the way. All the best with the bat mitzvah."

"Ah, yes. Appreciate it, Dave. Diane and I are really looking forward to it now it's definitely going to happen. We're blessed. Thanks to that new rabbi."

The delectable aromas of Shabbos wafted across Diane Goldstein's kitchen — red pepper soup, gefilte fish loaf, chocolate mousse cake — and drifted out over the dining table adorned with white cloth and candles. As she lifted the pan of challah from the oven, the front door swung open and Eliana rushed in, tossing her schoolbooks on the sofa and calling out, "I'm home, Mom," then hurrying down the hall toward her room. Mrs. Goldstein removed the challah from the pan and gently placed it on a wire rack to cool. She had just returned the hot pads to their wall pegs when the phone rang. After wiping her hands on the kitchen towel, she picked up the receiver.

Goldsteins … Yes, this is Diane … Oh, Leah! I didn't recognize your voice, dear. How nice you called! What a surprise! How's everything? … Good. Wonderful … Oh, we're fine here. Sammy is still busting his tail at the brokerage, set on landing that promotion. And Eliana is doing much better. Her grades are back up … Yes … In fact, she's having her bat mitzvah tomorrow morning. Didn't I write you? … Oh, that's right! Well, of course, you have no idea. It's a near miracle, Leah. I'm telling you, a miracle. The child went through so much. The shock, and the grief … No, he's in prison awaiting trial now. It was all such a sordid tragedy. So senseless! … Well, I'm not sure what all you knew. But Eliana met the young boy, Bobby, through a soccer club. And they were both auditioning for parts in a play at the Jewish Community Center … Yes, he was a Christian. That's right.

But Eliana fell head over heels. Her first big crush. He was waiting for her in front of the Center when this deranged maniac drove up, and started randomly shooting. And killed Bobby and his grandfather. Eliana arrived minutes later and witnessed the terror and commotion ... They don't know, Leah. He had ties to supremacists, but who knows? So wanton and heartless! Anyway, Eliana was devastated. She cried without ceasing. Began to question everything. Her faith. Her heritage. Refused to attend Shabbat ... No, she felt the bullets were really meant for her — and our people. That Bobby had died in her place. There was no consoling her ... No. Nothing ... I tell you, Leah, Sammy and I were at the end of our tether. But then heaven intervened ... Well, like I wrote you, they acquired a new rabbi at a neighboring synagogue. A handsome young man named Levine. Who'd grown up, of all places, in Jerusalem. His feet planted in the earth of our people. Such a warm personality and quick wit. Yet given to great compassion, too. One month he came to us to fill in for Rabbi Bernstein. And offered to counsel Eliana. I tell you, Leah, that was the beginning of the light coming back into our lives ... Absolutely. Heaven sent ... He was so gentle. So patient. He'd experienced the long struggle himself from deep inside. Seen the violence in his homeland. He spoke to her, Leah, straight from the heart. Went with her once to take flowers and pray at Bobby's grave. Wept with her. Then dried her tears. Soothed her wounded spirit with a balm of whispered hope. Such a mensch, that one. Gradually Eliana began coming back to herself. The first Shabbat she agreed to return to, he had her stand beside him as he read from the Torah. Little by little the guilt faded away and she reclaimed a forward view of life once more. A miracle, Leah, I tell you! We can never thank him enough ... Oh yes, that too was a most special incentive. His promising to be at her bat mitzvah. She's so excited about it all ... But, here I've cornered the conversation talking about us — what about you, Leah? When are you going to sell the house? ... I see. Yes ... When are you coming to visit? Our door is always open, you know ... I know, I know ... Well, all right. It's so good of you to call ... Yes, I'll tell Sammy hello for you, and Eliana too. She's in her room now ... Yes, Leah. All right then. Shalom.

Sammy looked up to see David step into the doorway,

his jacket draped over one arm.

"Well, got'em done. And I'm outta here," David said. "You're not working late on a Friday, are you?"

"Certainly not," Sammy replied. "I'm just wrapping things up. Gotta check off a couple things and I'm out the door myself."

"Okay. See you Monday."

"Right. Have a good one, Dave."

David departed down the hall and Sammy turned back to his desk. He picked up the Westenmar Communications folder and shoved it into a desk drawer, then looked out the window into the distance. The traffic along the expressway had grown heavy now. He sat a moment staring at the city beginning the transition from work day to evening, twisting his pen in his fingers. Three gulls drifted lazily above the water across his line of sight, the late afternoon sun lending a golden glow to their feathers.

Sammy reached over and picked up the framed picture at the side of his desk, a photo of Eliana posing on her bicycle, smiling gleefully, a daisy in her hair. The picture had been taken when life was a bubble of happiness and discovery and innocence. Before the arrival of merciless reality — which always must come sooner or later. At least we were still given moments to cherish, he thought. To fling back defiantly into reality's face. And a camera to photograph some of those moments, as he would the bat mitzvah tomorrow, to cling to and hold close throughout whatever might come next. And, yes, still some flicker of compassion amidst an unforgiving world, as evidenced by the commitment of a young rabbi.

Sammy lifted the phone receiver, took a deep breath and punched in the number. Then waited for an answer.

Shelby? Goldstein here again. Glad I caught you … Yeah … Listen, there's been some developments here. About that Westenmar deal. Uhhhh … Well … Shelby, some deep pockets came in late today and bought up the balance of the issue. Uhhhh. Cleaned out the shares ... That's right. The offering is closed ... Yeah, it's done. So, if you've written a check, tear it up. And pitch the paperwork into the wastebasket. Sorry 'bout that ... Okay? ... Now, not to worry, Shelby. There'll be other deals rolling down the pike. I'll keep you in mind ... Sure thing ... No sweat, okay? ... Remember, I'm lookin' out for you, buddy. I'll be in touch.

Sammy placed the receiver back on the cradle, stood up and stretched his arms outward. Well, the big man wouldn't like it, shaving off the nonaccredited little guys to save their skin, but Sammy'd live with it. He'd make it wash. Sometimes Kretzheimer pushed it too far, just counting the dollars and not the flesh. Always the dollars against the minutes. Five, ten, fifteen, twenty, twenty-five, thirty, thirty-five.

"Three Calls and a New Rabbi"

MARK SCHEEL was born and raised on a Kansas farm back when there were little country schools and life was a flowing river that more or less made sense. He's been a laborer, construction worker, topographic survey assistant, laundryman, Red Cross field representative, disaster relief worker, college English instructor, retail clerk, library information specialist, editor, poet, and writer. He has been published in numerous periodicals such as *Kansas City Voices* and *Artifact*, and his 1997 book, *A Backward View: Stories and Poems*, was chosen for the J. Donald Coffin Memorial Book Award.

He says: "I've always admired the writing of Dorothy Parker and that's why this competition caught my eye. An actual tragedy here in Kansas City lent itself well to the competition. I've also always admired Hemingway and enjoyed the challenge of writing in the difficult objective point of view of which he was a master."

Skip Counting

PLEASE, GOD, let him telephone me now. I left my message over an hour and 17 minutes ago. I know I did it right this time. I listened to his robot voice through all of the options because the menu had changed (which it hadn't), pressed "2" for Animal Control, and told him my story after the beep. It shouldn't take this long on a Tuesday at 5:34 pm in September, but I'm new here and maybe things are different.

"It's OK," I tell the dog. "You're safe now."

I try to stop staring at the telephone. I need to change and catch the bus to work. I'm new and can't be late again. And I'm not supposed to have a pet. The dog, a scruffy little fella with squat legs and an old man's fuzzy face, tries to squirm off my lap again. I check his tags for a name.

"Skip."

That's not correct. This dog's real name is Mr. Scraps. I fiddle with his collar, a thin leather band with studs, and pop it open. Mr. Scraps' entire body shakes, the same way Coco used to after a bath or walk in the rain. I kiss the top of his head and drop the collar to the floor.

It's then that I notice the blood on my knee and the tear in my shorts. I put Mr. Scraps down and walk to the kitchen for a paper towel. I fold it in half and run it under cold water. Mr. Scraps runs to the closed balcony door and sits, glancing over at me expectantly.

"I bet you want a treat."

I dab the quarter-sized patch of blood on my knee. It

was the fence that did it. A little too high for the street. Someone should tell the neighborhood association. Unsafe, both top and bottom. That's how I first met Mr. Scraps, his tiny paw poking out from under that terrible fence and feeling around for a way out, looking for freedom.

I find Coco's water bowl and fill it for Mr. Scraps, who waits at the door whining. Coco loved loved loved a hot dog, so I slice one into tiny pieces.

"Who wants a treat?"

Mr. Scraps takes a piece of hot dog, then another and another. "That's enough, you greedy little piggie."

The telephone continues not to ring, and out on the less busy street, I know the number 12 bus is getting closer. My uniform feels crinkly new and smells like chemicals. I put on the shirt first and sigh. I really miss wearing shorts, even if they tear too easily. Mr. Scraps looks up at me, places a paw on my foot, and tilts his head up to lick my bleeding knee. Coco had never done that. Neither had Fifi, Scout, or Mustard. I really like this Mr. Scraps. And for the first time, I think about the boy.

He was young, maybe seven years old, with tiny fists and red hair. His real name is Willie, but I'm sure his family and that bully butler call him Kevin, Dennis, or Corey because they don't know any better. Willie didn't see me at first. He sat, back to me, at a child-sized picnic table in the backyard as I slipped over the fence, following my old mailbag to the mulch-covered ground.

Mr. Scraps saw his chance and ran over. The little guy was so excited that he forgot to use his soft mouth and sank his teeth right into my hand. I must have yelped with surprise because it was then that Willie turned around and saw me. He squinted and shook his head, as if trying to clear the sight of me from his eyes. I remained.

Mr. Scraps turned his attention to the mailbag, sniffing the strap and burrowing his nose into its folds. He was ready to go, so I scooped him up. Willie took two steps off the patio into grass with a bright-colored floppy notebook dangling from his hand. Three stories of house loomed behind him. A sprinkler head poked out next to his left foot. I pictured it jumping to life and soaking him.

"You're not our mailman," he said.

"Person," I said back. "Mail*person*."

"You're not our mailperson."

"Not yet. I'm testing the route to see if I like it."

Willie cocked his head, mouth upturned. He was either thinking or pretending to think. "Do you like it?"

"I don't like this fence so much," I said, shifting the mailbag to drop the dog in. "And this dog doesn't seem very happy here."

"I thought mailmen hated dogs."

"Mail*person*." I shook my head. "Who told you that? We love dogs. That's why when we see a sad dog, we have to investigate. It part of the job."

Willie frowned. I glanced at the house. Someone, probably a nanny or maid, passed through the kitchen and stopped. I only saw a silhouette, not the direction it faced. I slid the dog into the bag. Mr. Scraps was heavier than I'd thought he'd be. He whimpered. This made me think that he might be OK here with Willie, the silhouette, and the lousy fence.

But then Willie started talking about math. It took me a second to get that. He kept saying *something* skip *something* over and over, then I noticed the numbers and symbols on the cover of his floppy notebook. I like math. I do a lot of it at work now, counting change back to customers the proper way. Nobody else does it anymore but me. I saw the silhouette in the window shift so I took a step backward, feeling for the fence. Willie was crying by now, still talking about math.

"You're doing skip counting, right? That's easy. You want a trick?"

"What?" Willie wiped his eyes with his sleeve and snorted up a nostril of snot. Little boys are gross.

"It's a song, Willie. Just sing it. Sing the numbers."

I started singing the "Numbers by Five" song. That's not its real name. Maybe it doesn't have one. I don't know where I learned it. Mr. Scraps squirmed and rolled over in the bag, which I hadn't thought possible given the space.

"It goes 'Five, ten, fifteen, twenty, twenty-five, thirty,'" I said, bending over to let the dog out.

That's when the shouting started.

"Hey! What the fuck are you doing?" A butler in jogging shorts and a t-shirt stood on the patio and then started running our way. "Jacob, get away from him! Go!"

Mr. Scraps stayed in the bag and didn't say a peep as I swung it over the fence. The butler was still yelling and Willie, even though I'd given him the secret to skip counting, hit me with his tiny fists. I vaulted over the fence and sprinted down the alley, across the busy street to the less busy street, through the parking lot with the shopping carts that hate me, and up the stairs to my apartment. The whole time with the little dog tight against my belly.

Mr. Scraps circles a spot on the carpet five times before turning himself into a sleeping round little donut dog. I put some water in a little soup bowl and the rest of the hot dog on plate on the kitchen floor on top of some newspapers.

The phone rings first, and Mr. Scraps doesn't care. He dozes away on the carpet. He doesn't even wake up when the knocking on the door starts or the yelling. Mr. Scraps is a good dog.

I wait for something to stop. I can't be on the telephone and at the door at the same time. I'm just one person, and I'm trying really hard. I did good things today. I saved Mr. Scraps. I taught Willie math.

Five, ten, fifteen, twenty, twenty-five, thirty, thirty-five….

"Skip Counting"

ROBERT ATKINSON is a Canadian citizen living in Maryland, in the United States. He is a content strategist and has a novel, *The Book of Catches*, available on Amazon.

He says: "This story is based on a friend's aunt who repeatedly 'rescued' perfectly healthy and cared-for dogs from people's backyards. It was interesting to play with a character who always believes they're right and heroic in the face of overwhelming evidence to the contrary. I was aiming for funny, but I think it landed somewhere a bit darker (in a good way)."

The Breaking Point

"PLEASE, GOD, let him telephone me now," Ruth said wringing her hands together as she sat at her kitchen table. Nearly nine years had passed and she'd not heard a word from youngest son James in all that time, and yet earlier in the day, she'd received that strange desperate message on her answering machine saying he would try to call back later. Of all days to get her hair permed, it just had to come on the day he decided to call. How ironic and cruel it was. She wanted to pull her hair out.

How many times in one's life does God give you a second chance? she thought. She covered her face, squeezing her eyes tightly, replaying that day over and over again in her head. She glanced up at the clock above the stove, 5:23. Paul would be home expecting his supper promptly at 6:00. The aroma of meatloaf baking in the oven filled the kitchen. She stood and walked over to the stove. Steam billowed from the green beans as they boiled away in a pan. She took a spoon, added a dollop of bacon grease and stirred. As she opened the oven door, a wave of heat rushed by her face. The grease crackled and popped atop the golden brown meat. She turned down the heat and let it rest. Meatloaf used to be his favorite, she thought.

She sat back down beside the answering machine and pressed play once again. At first there was a long pause, "Mom, Dad, this is James. Uh, I don't know if you'll ever get this message or if you want to respond … uh, I'm in trouble and, oh fuck it, maybe I'll call back later…."

The tears came again after hearing the despair in his

voice. It was different than she remembered, deeper in tone. He was barely fourteen when she last heard his voice. She pushed the play button again and sighed.

She glanced up at the clock again. "Oh, God, please, Paul will be home soon, let him telephone me now," she whispered, rubbing her hands through her graying hair. She stood, placed dinner rolls on a pan and buttered the tops. She donned her mitts and pulled the golden brown meatloaf from the oven and sat it on the table. About that time she heard her husband's car pull into the driveway. She quickly popped out the cassette tape, placed it in a drawer and replaced it with a new one.

Ruth fixed her hair and wiped the tears from her eyes as she took a deep breath and stood up straight. The front door opened, and Ruth put on a fake smile as she stirred the beans.

Paul, a stocky middle-aged man with balding red hair, tossed his fedora onto the hat rack, then took off his jacket and hung it on a hook by the door. He sniffed the air and smiled, "Mmm, I smell meatloaf."

Ruth walked into the living room, wearing her fake smile. "Honey, how was your day?" Paul rolled his eyes and grunted. "That bad, huh?" she said, lightly kissing his cheek. "Dinner's almost ready."

"Work was fine, except I got into some argument with George Hall over some lesbian at work. George accused me of being a bigot when I said that God had a special place in hell for fags. He knew I was right," Paul said, loosening his tie and slipping off his dress shirt.

"I best get back in the kitchen and check on the rolls," Ruth said, trying to change the subject.

Paul followed her into the kitchen and sat down at the table in his white tank top undershirt, his big beer belly poking out from under it. Paul picked up the newspaper without saying a word, browsing the headlines.

Ruth served her husband his plate of food and then fixed

herself one and sat beside him at the kitchen table. She looked at the clock that read 5:57, and then at the telephone. Her knees were knocking together under the table as she picked at her food. Paul folded the paper, placing it on the table beside his plate, and dug into his meatloaf without looking up.

Suddenly the phone rang. Ruth's head snapped up as she dropped her fork on her plate. She rushed to answer it, her heart beating wildly. "Hello?" she said timidly. She let out a huge sigh and said, "Paul, it's George from work."

Paul rolled his eyes and furrowed his brow. He wiped his hands on his napkin and walked to the phone. "George here. Yeah...?" he grumbled.

Ruth sat back down and picked up her fork. She glanced up at the clock. Her stomach was all in knots. "Please, God, hang up the phone," she thought to herself. Finally Paul hung up the phone and came back to the table and sat down. "What was that all about?" she said.

"Ah, it was just George inviting us to go bowling with him and Ellen tomorrow night. I think that's his way of apologizing for the argument he started at lunch. I guess he realizes that I was right after all," said Paul, grabbing another roll. He looked up and cocked his head to the side, eyeing Ruth curiously. "Something's different about you," he said.

Ruth's eyes got big. "What do you mean?" she said nervously.

"You look different somehow. Did you do something with your face?"

"Oh yeah, I got a new perm today. Do you like it?" she said, patting her hair.

"Yeah, I suppose," he said, digging back into his food.

Ruth sighed and took a bite of her meatloaf. She stared back at the clock and picked at her food as they ate in silence.

Suddenly the phone rang again. Startled, Ruth dropped her fork on the floor. Just as she was getting up, Paul said,

"I'll get this, Ruth. People should know better not to call during suppertime." He marched over to the phone and picked up the receiver. "Hello, hello? ... Who is this? George, if that's you, you shouldn't keep calling at supper," he said angrily.

Ruth's eyes widened and she gasped. "Paul, who is it?"

"Who is this? ... *Who?*" Paul's brow furrowed again and he gritted his teeth. "You know better not to call this number again," he said angrily.

"Paul, who is it!" she said more forcefully, getting up from her seat.

"*No*, you can't speak to her ... She doesn't want to talk to you," he said, putting his arm out to block Ruth from talking. Paul muffled the receiver against his chest and motioned for Ruth to sit back down. He put the receiver to his ear again and smirked. "Listen to me. I don't care if you're in trouble. When you sin against God, you'll have to answer to Him yourself. Please, don't you ever call back here again," he said and hung up the phone.

Ruth sat down rigid, staring at her plate. Her eyes glazed over with tears. She clenched her fists into tiny little balls that rested upon her bony knees. At that moment she wanted to kill him. She shook with rage. Paul sauntered back to the table and took his seat. He put his elbow on the table and rested his chin in his hand, staring at her as she sat there motionless. "Your food's gonna get cold. You better eat it," he said calmly, raising an eyebrow with a slight grin.

"I'm not hungry," she mumbled under her breath. *Five, ten, fifteen, twenty, twenty-five...* she counted in her thoughts.

"What did you make for dessert? You did make dessert, didn't you?" he said, grabbing another dinner roll.

She sat silent. He repeated the question and cocked his head, waiting for a response. "I made a chocolate cake. It's in the cupboard," she said coldly.

"Aren't you gonna get me a piece?" he said, holding his fork in his hand with a smirk.

She stood up, walked to the cupboard and put the cake on the counter. She grabbed a saucer and a sharp knife from the drawer and took a deep breath. She stood facing the cake and closed her eyes tightly. *Five, ten, fifteen, twenty, twenty-five, thirty….* she counted and sighed, letting her chin fall to her chest. She cut a slice of cake, put it on a saucer and placed it on the table in front of Paul. He dug into it without looking up.

Ruth took her unfinished plate to the sink and scraped the food into the trash. She quietly took Paul's finished plate and began washing dishes as Paul grabbed a beer from the refrigerator and headed to the living room. She heard him turn on the TV.

While Paul was watching TV, Ruth picked up the receiver and pushed redial. She nervously watched to see if Paul might come back. She let the phone ring on the other end almost twenty times before someone picked up. "Hello," she whispered.

"Hello, who is this?" a voice answered back.

"James? James, is that you?" she whispered as her eyes filled with tears.

"Nah, this is Bill. I just picked up the phone."

"Where is this phone located?"

"Ma'am, this is a pay phone on the corner of Camp and St. Joseph here in New Orleans. Are you expecting someone to be here?" he said.

"No, I suppose not. Goodbye," she said, hanging up the phone. Her heart sank as a numbness crept over her body. She reached into the drawer, pulled out the cassette tape, put it in the answering machine and pushed play. She listened to the recording over and over.

"Ruth, bring me another beer," Paul yelled.

She opened the refrigerator, took a can of Miller Lite out of the case, marched into the living room and handed it to Paul as he sat in his reclining chair. He took the beer from her hand and stuck his foot out, blocking her from returning to the kitchen. He chuckled and said, "What's got into you all of a sudden? You pissed about James, huh?"

"I don't see why you wouldn't let me talk to our son. I hadn't heard a thing in all those years," she pleaded. "We may never hear from him again."

"Now you're gonna start crying. Boo hoo hoo!" he said, mocking her. "James dishonored me by choosing to be gay. I wasn't gonna allow that shit in this house. Oh, hell no! He committed a crime against God and nature," Paul yelled as his face flushed with rage.

"He was just a child," she cried. "What sort of parents do that to their own child?"

"God-fearing parents. I did what I had to do. You need to forget him, Ruth. He chose this life and now he has to live it without our help," he said, lying back down in his chair.

Ruth turned and stormed off toward the kitchen. She sat down on a kitchen chair and stared blankly at her hands.

Later that night, Ruth looked up at the clock, which said 12:49. All was quite in the house except for the hum of the refrigerator. Paul had consumed eleven beers and stumbled off to bed a few hours earlier. Ruth played that tape over and over as she sat, shaking. Her hands bled as she squeezed her fingernails deep into her palms. *Five, ten, fifteen, twenty*... — when she reached a hundred she opened her eyes and stared at the large chef knife lying on the counter.

Ruth calmly rose from her seat and picked up the knife. The shaking ended as she walked toward the stairs. Paul's snoring could be heard at the bottom of the staircase. As she slowly climbed the steps she whispered softly to herself, "Five, ten, fifteen, twenty, twenty-five, thirty, thirty-five…."

"The Breaking Point"

JACK SLATER is a general laborer from Washington State, in the United States. He graduated from Berea College, enjoys gardening and hiking, and is currently working on a novel. "The Breaking Point" is his first published story.

He says: "The story was inspired by a dear friend named James, who had been living on the streets since the age of 14 as a male prostitute. He had been kicked out of his home for being gay."

Josh Lefkowitz

My Final Lover

PLEASE, GOD, let him telephone me now.
Or else I'll know he's gone off with another.
And this will mark my end with love. Somehow,
I know it's true. He'll be my final lover.
Lord, I pray to you — make the line ring!
And let that ring be transferred to my finger!
It little profits this most idle thing
That you should let uncertainty still linger.
But if our love must end here, so will I.
Thus explains the handgun, and the bullet.
I'll count to seven, in increments of five.
And then, if still no call, I'll do it. I know it.
God, it's in your hands. Shall I stay alive?
Five, ten, fifteen, twenty, twenty-five, thirty, thirty-five.

"My Final Lover"

JOSH LEFKOWITZ is a legal practice specialist from Brooklyn, New York. His poems have been published in *Electric Literature*, *The Huffington Post*, *Washington Square Review*, *Barrelhouse*, *Shooter Literary Magazine* (UK), *Southword Journal* (Ireland), and many other places.

He says: "I felt a familiarity with the despair of the first line, as I definitely know what it's like to be hoping and pleading to some deity for the phone to ring (or a text message reply in today's preferred communication methods). Then, eyeing the final line, I tried to think of the most dramatic situation that might warrant the counting. I (aim to) write a poem every day, so this was a great opportunity to step outside the autobiographical impulse and work within Parker's provided constraints. She's a real hero of mine."

Underwire

PLEASE, GOD, let him telephone me now.

Okay, maybe not *right* now. Not here at the Walmart. Not while Jeannie was flattened against the wall of bras waiting for the woman in the motorized cart to roll by. She surveyed the names of colors — electric blue, lilac lullaby, sunset orange, mocha, snow. Promises dangled from their labels — allure, uplift, contour, support or comfort. Allure in the sunset or comfort in the snow? *They're only words.* Jeannie plucked off five bras and hoped no one noticed her hands shaking.

Practically since the beginning Bobby had been telling Jeannie that she thought too much. "Like for one thing, it isn't normal to have feelings about other people's groceries," he said. So most of the time Jeannie kept that sort of thing to herself. But she wished she could tell him about the tube socks, canned pears, wine coolers, highway emergency flares and a sequined camisole in the motorized-cart-lady's basket. If it weren't for the canned pears the combination might've seemed exciting in a potentially dangerous way. Jeannie would've liked to tell him about the tiny old lady caressing satin panties with her crooked fingers. Her hands moved from bikinis to briefs and back again. Jeannie wanted to ask the lady what she was thinking. The Walmart lingerie aisle did not deserve her subtle smile, the far-away look in the lady's eyes. She must've been imagining some other place or time, probably somewhere long gone. But as Bobby had said, "Nobody gives a shit about stuff like that."

Jeannie tried not to make eye contact.

Better if she didn't answer the phone anyway. A security guard with "Bella" on her name tag was stationed at the dressing room entrance. She would hear everything.

Jeannie made sure that the Walmart gift card Bobby had given her for her birthday was still in her wallet. Her coworkers at the call center hadn't been as enthusiastic about Bobby's choice as Jeannie pretended to be. The new girl on the other side of the partition had gone so far as to tell Jeanie that she shouldn't get too hopeful. "Now, if it'd been for Victoria's Secret, that'd be different."

Jeannie stared at her phone wondering if she'd accidentally made some kind of change that caused it to ignore all incoming calls. Phones were like that. Some random touch could erase everything you'd carefully set up.

Perspiration trickled down her sides but Jeannie wouldn't curse. Not out loud.

Maybe Jeannie did think too much, but her mother had declared Jeannie the most practical of her daughters. It was true. Jeannie quit visiting creative and affordable bridal websites the same day Bobby gave her a ride to the car repair shop. He could not or would not explain the reek of patchouli on the passenger seat or the tube of dark red lip gloss rolling around in the cup holder of his beloved Mustang. On and off she returned to those questions and added more, like about his sudden interest in bowling alone at odd hours. But after they celebrated her pay raise at the Red Lobster Jeannie decided to stop asking. *Everything was fine.*

Jeannie hung up the cheery cherry underwire without bothering to try it on. What was she thinking? She'd never be able to wear it under white. Four more bras to go. Five items were allowed in the dressing room and she had counted them off for the blank faced security guard before stepping behind the curtain.

Jeannie wasn't entirely clear how she'd come to be at the

Walmart, where she'd parked or why she'd walked past every single clearance rack on her way to the lingerie aisle. But it hadn't been an ordinary day. Around lunch time Bobby had called. "We need to talk," he'd said. Jeannie's feet had gone cold and her hands instantly started sweating but she pulled it together enough to say, "That'll be just fine, I'll come by your place." She clicked the button before he could say anything else.

Maybe in a month or so they'd be sitting on the deck off Bobby's third floor apartment and they'd laugh about the whole thing. On their first date, four years ago, Bobby invited her out to the deck, rocked back on his heels, stretched out his arms and announced, "I've got the best view." She hadn't been sure if he was kidding or not. Railroad tracks fronted a line of warehouses that looked like bleak versions of those towering plateaus in old Westerns — the high flat places where the bad guys stealthily lurked. The deck sagged in places and the wood was so rough Jeannie never failed to get a splinter. But still, Bobby loved the deck.

Someday they'd look down at the cracked concrete slab beneath it and say, "Remember that time?" And they'd chuckle. Not a real laugh but the private kind that keeps everybody else out of the joke.

She decided to count by twos if the phone rang and only if she got to twenty would she look at the number.

Maybe without intending to, they'd save the story for special occasions. Maybe on their anniversary he'd say, "Remember that day?" and Jeannie would gently trace her finger across his forehead and sigh. Bobby would lighten the mood and say something cute about Jeannie not knowing her own strength.

Two, four, six, eight, ten, twelve, Jeannie cheated but didn't recognize the number so she ignored it. The tag in the back of the moss green bra felt like a knife slicing into her skin and Jeannie heard herself cursing loudly as she tried to get the thing turned around. Eons ago her mother had demonstrated the maneuver of letting down the straps then sliding the bra around so the clasps were in the front. But Jeannie had too much sweat covering too much skin to perform the trick with any grace.

Practical but uncoordinated Jeannie. She had scars in unlikely places. The thin white line bisecting her lower lip was from climbing over the back seat of the station wagon and landing on her face in the gravel parking lot of the Italian restaurant. She'd been six and for years afterwards her stepfather would jokingly remind Jeannie to put her feet on the ground before her face.

Jeannie had to consciously work at things other people could do in their sleep and that, along with thinking too much was her problem. But hadn't her boss given her the raise because she'd started adding a personal touch to her calls? Before the customer could click off she'd find some connection, their name sounded familiar or she'd ask them about the weather wherever they were. All that unspoken thinking spilled onto strangers probably sitting alone in living rooms in towns she'd never heard of.

The phone buzzed again and she decided to switch to increments of threes. *Three, six, nine, twelve.* With one breast out of the white satin bra she glanced at the number. It was the sheriff's department. Probably a misdial.

"Ma'am? You alright in there?" the security guard asked. Her voice sounded kind but wary.

Jeannie liked the white satin. And she thought she understood why the old lady with the gnarled fingers seemed so happy. *Fifteen, eighteen, twenty-one.*

If it hadn't cooled off enough to sit outside things would've come out differently. If it hadn't been such a spectacular sunset maybe they'd have stayed inside. But a streak of almost greenish light splayed across Bobby's head, changing his hair from plain brown to a color close to auburn. And as if he felt the wonder of it all he laughed, threw his head back, stuck the long neck bottle into his mouth and swallowed all sixteen ounces of beer without choking. *People loved Bobby.*

Without even turning around, Bobby had hopped up on the railing. He balanced his ass halfway on, halfway off, his legs spread apart. It was then that an idea arose in Jeannie's mind. She saw the idea in the form of a PowerPoint slide from work. It was typed in a plain black typeface on a yellow background like a warning label on a corrosive chemical — "*Everything he does reminds you of what you'll never be.*"

"You ought not to sit up there like that. It's not safe," Jeannie said the same way she had plenty of times before.

"There you go again," he said, "thinking too much."

Jeannie was deciding between the sunshine yellow lace push up and the white satin. The white made her feel substantial, the yellow demure. *You can't have everything.* A Bee Gee's song was playing and she speculated whether there was anybody in the store old enough to know the words. It was long past supper time.

The sound of carts colliding drifted over from housewares and Jeannie sunk onto the spindly metal stool. *Bobby would probably like the yellow.* But then she remembered the concrete and the specific thwack sound his skull had made.

Jeannie stood up, yanked a barely used tissue from her purse and wiped the wetness from her face. She squared her shoulders and decided to switch to increments of five. If asked, few people would say that three was a good number, too complicated. The phone buzzed.

Five, ten, fifteen, but maybe she hadn't given enough consideration to the peach cotton bra. It reminded Jeannie of the training bra her mother gave her on her twelfth birthday. Jeannie had asked for a cowgirl set that included a white straw hat, a red bandana and almost real looking metal pistols that made a clicking sound when you pulled the trigger. "You're a big girl now," her mother had said.

Did everybody else already know that bones make a nauseating sound when they break?

The guard's meaty hand with tangerine fingernails parted the curtain slightly. "Ma'am, there are other folks needing the dressing room." Why had Bobby been laughing? Had Jeannie asked about the patchouli scent again? It clung to him like a skunk-sprayed dog. Maybe she'd spoken this thought aloud and he'd found it funny.

Jeannie's voice sounded like a pre-recorded message, "Yes, sorry, I'm almost done." She leaned over and let her breasts fall into the cups the way you're supposed to. The peach didn't stab into her sides or dig into her shoulders. But a few minutes of watching yourself in the mirror wasn't the same as real life and the bra wasn't on sale. Jeannie wanted to test the peach by moving around the way she would at work, adjusting her headset or reloading the printer but her hands wouldn't move. "Inert," that was the word for it. Not moving, also not dangerous.

"Ma'am, the store's going to close pretty soon," the security guard said.

Remembering her practical nature, Jeannie forced her hands to respond to her will. She worked at removing the peach bra as if it was an intricately designed puzzle.

The phone vibrated itself off of the metal stool and continued buzzing as it spun in circles on the floor. Jeannie reached for the phone slowly as if to reassure a cornered reptile that she meant it no harm. *Where were my hands when Bobby's body left the railing?*

"Everything okay in there, ma'am?"

Five, ten, fifteen, twenty, twenty-five, thirty, thirty-five.

"Underwire"

GRACE KIMBERLY TEEPLES is a museum gallery associate from Virginia, in the United States. She alternates between writing fiction and altering books by taking them apart and remaking them into visual art — another kind of literary taxidermy. "Underwire" is her first published story.

She says: "I read the Dorothy Parker lines and something happened that only happens once in a blue moon. The story arrived fully formed. My job was not to question why the lingerie aisle came to mind. Two things came together, the use of visual metaphor in art and my love of reading and writing mysteries."

Sugar Skulls

"PLEASE, GOD, let him phone me now," she prayed, hugging the phone to her chest like a rosary. "Give me a sign."

Because if he called, it meant this was all real. It meant she wasn't crazy.

Maya hurried down the sidewalk, her arms tucked tight against her ribs as she shouldered her way through the crowded street. She was moving against the flow of the parade, jostling her way past flower-festooned skeletons and devils in flowing lace. The women wore their brightest dresses, men their finest charro suits. A few stared at Maya as she hurried past them, a kid all by herself, plain and frazzled in dirty jeans and blouse.

She didn't care. She didn't have time to.

As the crowd began to thin, she paused to count the tiny sugar skulls growing smeared and sticky in her palm. They were no larger than mice skulls, white and glistening, each with a dye-painted grin and flower. Each one represented five minutes to save her dead father's soul. Panic flooded through her. Fifty minutes left — was that all?

Maya hurried through the last dregs of the parade. Her hands were crowded with the phone, the sugar skulls, the thin straps from the heavy backpack on her shoulders. The streets were littered with trampled hats, bits of tissue paper, the odd blossom flattened into the cobblestones. But she only had eyes for the way ahead. At last the road was clear enough and she began to run. She had to get to the graveyard. She had to —

The phone buzzed in Maya's hand and she gasped, nearly dropping it. An unregistered number. Just like before.

She jabbed at the green icon, swiping it aside, and pressed the phone against her ear. "Hello?"

"Hello, Maya," a soft voice said. "Having any luck?"

"I have it," she said, her voice cut short by her ragged breathing. "I'm on my way."

"Oh, *good.* Your father will be so relieved."

She ran, hearing her own breathing echoing back in the phone. She swallowed hard, her throat tight. "Can I talk to him?"

"Now, darling, you know the rules. We wouldn't want to let *those* slip, would we?"

No, she didn't. If there was one person in the universe she couldn't afford to let cheat her, it was him. But she hadn't talked to her father since his death last month. He had died without warning, without goodbyes. What harm would just a few final words do?

"I know you're very busy, my dear," the man said. "I won't keep you. *Buena suerte.*"

Maya struggled to breathe past the lump in her throat as the call ended, and then shoved the phone in her pocket, starting at a run down the littered pavement. She had her sign. There was no more time for wondering.

The parade was for tourists and scammers, with all its glitter and revelry. The real *Día de los Muertos* happened in the homes and in the cemeteries, at the altars and the gravestones. Night had fallen and a thousand candles were already lit on the hilltop ahead, just as they were in every graveyard in Mexico. She could picture her family at home, loading the altar with *offerendas* and memories before they would hurry to the family's mausoleum for the vigil. She had to be done before they arrived.

Would her family be celebrating if they realized where

her father was right now?

Maya didn't care. He was her father and she loved him. She knew his heart, and it wasn't meant for that place, no matter what he had done. She would do anything for him, even risk her own immortal soul. She glanced down at the sugar skulls in her sticky palm. Thirty, thirty-five, forty. *Forty minutes*. She ran a little faster.

The gates to the cemetery were wide and welcoming with candles dancing in the warm breeze. *Día de los Muertos* was the only night of the year when she could expect the mausoleum to be open, and it was nearly over. Tonight was her last chance. Her sweaty hand tightened around the candies. As long as she still had sugar skulls, she still had time. But they were rapidly disintegrating in her palm. Time was running out.

The mausoleum was cleaned and swept, draped with garlands of marigold and paper flowers. Painted skulls and framed photographs surrounded by unlit candles sat on a black draped bench in front of the door of the tomb.

Maya swallowed, the eyes of her ancestors staring back at her. Her grandmother smiled with crinkled eyes and Maya looked away. She stepped carefully around the bench and shouldered the door open.

It was cold and dim inside, the floor strewn with marigold petals, each crypt waiting with a single fresh candle. Maya brushed her fingers along the bronze plates as she passed them, each bearing a name she knew by heart. Her great-grandfather had commissioned the tomb, and there was only room for a few more. By the time Maya died, she'd have to find somewhere else to rest.

Her father was in the back, his casket resting among the few remaining niches. There was a space for Uncle Avelino and Aunt Maria, and a little room for Maya's mother. Her father's casket looked lonely all by itself. A small white candle sat on the niche beside his brass plate, ready to burn in his memory.

Maya set the remaining sugar skulls — *fifteen, twenty, twenty-five minutes* left now — in the niche beside her father's candle and wiped her slimy palm on the thigh of her pants. She slid the backpack from her shoulders and set it with a loud clank on the stone floor, opening the zipper.

The man on the phone had been clear. Yes, her father had done some very bad things, but he was not beyond redemption. Not if Maya was willing to help. The man gave her until the time of the graveyard vigils to obtain an indulgence for her father, to bring him the last rites he had died without. But it wasn't enough to simply ask the priest and say her prayers. Not while the man on the phone was involved.

He seemed bored. Why else make a game of it?

Maya lifted the things she needed out of her backpack, setting them on the marigold-strewn floor. A votive candle. A plastic bin with an unbroken holy wafer. A water bottle of sacramental wine. Her grandmother's rosary and Bible. Everything she needed to free her father. She winced to think of what the poor priest would say about all this, his grey eyes full of disappointment. But what else could she do? Her father needed her.

She pulled the final two items out of her backpack — a crowbar and a hammer.

Maya stood, facing her father's crypt. The surface was smooth marble, the bronze nameplate dark and peaceful in the dim light. Maya swallowed, sweat blooming along her spine.

She swung the hammer hard, smashing the thin plate of marble. Her father's name chipped off and disappeared into the marigolds. She hit it again, sick to her stomach, smashing it over and over until the marble crumbled and fell away.

Next was a sheet of metal, smooth and plain. Maya hit it at the corner with her hammer, warping the metal, and then wedged the tip of the crowbar under the edge. She glanced nervously back at the door of the mausoleum and then threw her weight against the crowbar.

Maya had been in a delirium of grief when the man on the phone had called, just as night was falling on the first day of *Día de los Muertos*. She had moved hesitantly, uncertainly. Had she dreamed the phone call? She wished she hadn't hesitated so much. She could have used the extra time. But the bag of sugar skulls had seemed endlessly full, and the man's claims endlessly improbable. Piece by piece, she had started to see, until the final call came to seal her belief.

If only it had come a little sooner.

She grunted, heaving against the crowbar, and wedged the tip a little further into the widening hole. She glanced at the sugar skulls — only three left — and braced a foot against the marble column running between niches. She pulled the crowbar with both hands, pushing against the column. The metal tore away from the corner, screeching against the edge of the marble, creeping open bit by bit, just wide enough for the crowbar, then just wide enough for her fingers, and then just wide enough to slide a hand through. She wrenched and twisted, sweat trickling through her hair and down her back, until the hole was wide enough to reach through. Maya paused, panting, and stared at the twisted sheet of metal.

The phone rang again and she jolted, dropping the crowbar. It clattered loudly off the lip of the niche and then dropped to the petal-muffled floor. She fumbled with her pocket, digging out her phone, and stared at the screen.

Mamá. Maya watched her mother's picture, tongue stuck playfully out at her, as the phone rang a third time. Maya had been ignoring her mother's calls all day. She had to be worried. Maya swallowed, her thumb hovering over the green icon.

Six rings. Seven.

It rang an eighth time and went to voicemail. Her mother

was going to kill her when all of this was over and she finally went slinking home again.

Maya couldn't ask her mother for help. She couldn't ask anyone, couldn't explain anything. Even asking the priest if she could have the wine and wafer was against the rules. So she had to sneak and steal. She had to disappear and leave her family worrying.

Besides, Maya knew what her mother thought of gambling. And when the stakes were more than just money, she couldn't imagine the words her mother would have on the matter.

Maya shoved the phone back in her pocket and wiped at her nose, glaring at the sugar skulls and then the hole. There were only two skulls left. Maya didn't have time for this. She fought down the sob rising in her throat and crouched among the petals.

She set the bottle and the bin at the base of the marble column and knelt, lighting the votive candle. She placed it in the open shelf below her father's and bowed her head, hands clasped beneath her chin. "Hail, Mary, full of grace," she prayed, her whisper flickering the candle flame.

It wasn't supposed to be like this. This was *Día de los Muertos*. She was supposed to be celebrating with her family. She was supposed to be welcoming beloved spirits home. But she wasn't. She was here instead, defiling her father, defiling the Holy Eucharist, defiling her own soul. Everything was wrong, everything was warped. But she didn't have a choice.

She wiped her cheeks, smearing streaks of sweat and sugar in with the tears, and choked, "Pray for us sinners, now and at the hour of our death. Amen."

The phone rang again. Maya grit her teeth against the ringtone. She swiped the red icon below her mother's picture and turned to the casket.

Before she could lose her nerve, she stood, picking up the crowbar, and jammed it into the seam between the lid and the bottom. The tip sank in easily and, with a twist, the lid knocked against the ceiling of the niche.

Maya held her breath, pulse pounding in her ears. Then she swallowed and released the crowbar, letting it hang between the lid and base. She leaned down and grabbed the bin, then cracked the seal and fished out the wafer without looking. She had to hurry, before the smell hit her, before the family arrived, before the sugar skulls ran out.

"Miguel Ángel Luis Gomez," Maya whispered, wishing she had written down the full prayer. "May God grant you pardon and peace. I – I absolve you of your sins." She didn't dare invoke the name of the Holy Trinity. God would strike her down on the spot.

Maya pushed the wafer through the gap, and then squeezed in the contents of the bottle as well. Then she tugged the crowbar out, letting the lid clap down into place.

She stared at the casket for several long moments. No lightning struck her. No flame engulfed her. All was quiet peace. Maya took a deep breath and mostly smelled marigolds.

A rising warmth spread through her chest, and she laughed suddenly.

She had done it. *She had done it.*

Maya placed the Bible and rosary on the coffin lid and scooped everything else into her backpack. She slung it up onto her shoulder, bursting out of the mausoleum and into the fresh, cool air. She smiled down at the families moving between gravestones.

Families. Her smile faded. She had to get home. Maybe if she arrived just as the family was leaving for the cemetery, her mother would leave her disappearance unpunished until morning. Full of hope, giddy with relief, Maya turned and ran toward the gates and home.

There was nobody at the house. Maya turned, peering down the sidewalk. Had she missed them somehow?

Uncertain, she started toward the cemetery again, pulling the phone out of her pocket.

Maya frowned at the screen. Her uncle had started calling her as well, about an hour ago. If Uncle knew she'd gone missing, the whole family did.

The phone pinged again, alerting her to another text message. She left it waiting with the other dozen her mother had already left. She would read them later. First, she had to check in before the search party grew any bigger.

Bracing herself, she pressed her mother's picture and the phone started to ring. She put it against her ear and waited.

"Maya?" a voice croaked in the phone.

Maya frowned. "Uncle? Is Mamá there?"

Her uncle started to cry, helpless, heaving sobs.

"I'm okay," she said quickly. "I'm on my way to the cemetery."

He didn't answer, his sobs joined by others in the background.

Coldness prickled along Maya's arms. She listened, waiting, waiting, but the explanation didn't come. Finally, she whispered, "Where's Mamá?"

It was too soon for another funeral. Everyone thought so. Maya especially. She clustered close to her brothers and her sister outside the mausoleum as the men slid their mother in beside their father, his marble sheet and bronze name plate neatly replaced after being vandalized on the last night of *Día de los Muertos*.

Maya knew all the motions. Knew all the words. She watched everything from a distance, the sounds muffled and hollow. She stared at the ground as friends and relatives trickled away through the graveyard, until finally her Aunt Maria herded her siblings away and Uncle Avelino took up a post down by the cemetery gates, waiting until she was done.

Done. She didn't even know what that meant. Done what?

She stood in the doorway for a long time, staring back at her parents. If her mother hadn't been out looking for Maya, she would still be alive. If she hadn't been dialing Maya when that truck ignored the traffic light, she would still be alive.

Her phone rang, loud in the silence, and she startled. Then her shoulders tensed angrily. She was certain she'd turned it off. Who would be calling her now? Why couldn't they leave her alone?

It rang seven times, then eight.

Then nine, and ten.

Maya frowned. It never rang this long.

She pulled the phone from her jacket and looked at the screen.

An unlisted number. And it was still ringing.

Maya swallowed. Then she thumbed the green icon and pressed the phone to her ear, whispering, "Hello?"

"Hello, Maya," the man on the phone said, and cold rushed across her skin. "My sincerest condolences."

Her voice was hoarse and flat, like a stranger's. "What do you want?"

"I'd like to propose another wager."

Maya's heart thudded painfully. "No. I did everything you said. It's over."

"Yes, your father is quite safe. He sends his thanks."

The pain spread through her chest, piercing the hollow in her heart. "Then who — "

"*You*, Maya," he said gently. "*Your* soul."

Her ribs ached from so much crying, so many held breaths. Finally, she whispered, "You — you said I —"

"I said that if you completed the task, with your own soul as a wager, that your father's soul would be free. And you did. But think what you did to accomplish it. It's not your father's soul I own now. It's yours. Just imagine how concerned your poor mother was."

She shook her head, staring sightlessly into the mausoleum. "No. You can't. Not her."

"You chose for your father. She chose for you. Such a devoted family."

"But —"

"You're wasting time. Turn around."

She did as she was told, and her eyes fell to the stone bench in front of the mausoleum door. A small pile of candies sat in the middle of it, black eyes staring from white faces.

Tiny little sugar skulls.

"Since you already know what to do, I'm afraid I can't give you as much time as before."

She shook her head with growing horror, staring down at the skulls. Again. She had to do it all again. The very thing that had killed her mother.

"Your mother is counting on you, Maya. *Buena suerte.*"

The phone slipped from her limp fingers. Against her will, Maya took the two lurching steps to the bench and stumbled to her knees. With leaden fingers, she began to count the sugar skulls, tallying up what little time she had, even as her mind fought against it.

She couldn't do this. Not again.

Please, God…

Five, ten, fifteen, twenty, twenty-five, thirty, thirty-five….

"Sugar Skulls"

JILL NICOLE MARCOTTE is an author from Alaska, in the United States. She plays rugby and teaches children how to bake French pastries. A fluent liar since birth, she writes fantasy, supernatural, horror, sci-fi, and whatever else catches her fancy. She has ben published in online magazines, competitions, and podcasts, including *GlassFire Magazine*, *Blood Moon Rising Magazine*, *Campfire Tales Anthology*, and *Tales to Terrify*.

She says: "My husband is my muse, which may be a little unfair since this story is not a nice one. I assure you, he is a very nice man, and incredibly patient with my pinging story ideas off the side of his head like a sounding board, then forcing him to read several drafts, insisting *yes, this ending actually is good enough* before realizing that *no, maybe it's not*, making him read several more drafts, and then wordlessly not cooking dinner. Like I said, a very nice and patient man."

Jocelyn Hoyle

Still Movement

PLEASE, GOD, let him telephone me now. Please, God, please. He can't still be in that meeting. He must have got my voicemails by now. I need to get to hospital. Now. *Right now.*

My bent knees are protruding from the hip-height water like two pointy mountain peaks. The three-quarter bathtub is too short to accommodate my outstretched legs. Bending forwards to rest my head on my knees, I feel a warm ripple of relief as the pain subsides. But nothing can conquer the crippling sense of dread. It's the second time in twelve months I've been in labour. Memories of the first time still torment me.

This time is different. With each contraction, I can feel my baby moving inside me, edging a little closer towards daylight. This time, my own hormones are doing the work. This time, the pain will be worth it. This time, there will be a living, moving, crying baby at the end of it all. This time will definitely be different. I just need to get to hospital. Please, God, please. He has to phone me now. Please, let him phone. Please, please.

Please, God, let me keep this baby. Let this baby make it. Yes, I know, last time was just unlucky. It was just one of those things; highly unusual; a rare occurrence. It won't happen again. I know, I know. Oh, God, I'm not blaming you. Really, I'm not. I'm sure you had your reasons. Perhaps you wanted my father to have a grandchild. He was a good man, a real gentleman. It wasn't his fault the car was speeding. He definitely looked right and left before he crossed. He would have been a wonderful grandfather, but he never got the chance. I agree, I totally agree, he deserved a little angel — I just didn't realise it would be my angel. But one angel is enough, God. You don't need to take another baby. This baby will be healthy and this baby will be mine. It will all be different this time. But please, please, I need to get to hospital. Please, God, let him phone me now.

I remember the exact day that I felt something was wrong with my baby. The sharp, jerky movements inside my belly turned into occasional dull twitches. It was like the popcorn machine had stopped popping. The orchestra had lost its percussion. I lightly tapped my side a few times, then my stomach, then my side again, trying desperately to elicit a response. Then I tapped a bit harder, faster, more urgently. But still, all she could give me was a note or two, not her usual sonata.

It was a Friday afternoon when I found out that my baby was going to die. I left the office early, locking my filing cabinet for the first time in months. All my instincts told me that I might not be back for a while. My husband was ten minutes late for the specialist ultrasound appointment. By the time he arrived, the sonographer had already gone quiet. No more chit-chat about baby names. It was like the curtain coming down at the end of a show. Even in that darkened room, I could see the sparkle leave her eyes. I watched her smile disappear as she nervously bit her lower lip. And when she left the room to get the doctor, I knew that something was wrong.

The ultrasound report confirmed it. Although the fetal heart was beating at a normal rate and rhythm, its appearance was anything but normal. There was a 'large atrial septal defect' and the heart was much bigger than it should have been. My baby's heart was so big it was squashing her lungs. The placenta showed the 'typical ground glass appearance seen in fetal cardiac failure.'

The prognosis was not good. My baby would probably die within a matter of days, and the hospital ethics committee wanted her delivered dead, rather than alive. I didn't want to believe it. I hated the idea of other people determining her fate; just waiting for her to die. I went ahead and did the usual things. Swam my laps on Saturday morning; did the grocery shopping; filled up the car; went for a walk along the beach. Everywhere I went, random strangers kept asking me when the baby was due. Any day now, I replied. They wanted to know if I was excited. Very excited, I lied.

When I woke on the Tuesday morning, I knew that she was gone. An overwhelming feeling of emptiness enveloped me. I stared at the little pink flowers on the doona cover for what seemed like hours. They were the same mushroom pink as the lampshade. Then I stared at my belly for even longer. I was too numb to cry. The obstetrician suggested a 6pm appointment, the last of the day, so that I could avoid a waiting room full of happy, expectant mothers. As he squeezed the smooth, clear gel onto my abdomen, I already knew that this ultrasound would be different. No playful skip in the soundtrack as a fetal heartbeat was detected. No sound of galloping horses as it settled into a steady pulse. Just the loud, continuous whooshing sound of my own blood flow. At 36 weeks, my baby was dead.

This time is different. It's all completely different. As I lie here in the bath, I can feel a little foot digging into my side. I can feel a little hand punching my belly. Or perhaps that was a hiccup. What am I worrying about? There's no reason to be anxious. Everything is fine. There's nothing wrong with this baby. It won't be long now. It won't be long before I experience the euphoria of giving birth and the joy of becoming a hands-on mother; the mother of a living child. Please, God, let him phone me. Please, I need him here, now.

Oh, God, I really want this time to be different. No, I don't just want it — I *need* it. This time has to be different. You wouldn't let me go through that again. Maybe you had a good reason the first time, but not this time. It would just be cruel to take another baby from me. You've already tested my faith, more than once. You don't need to test it again. You need to make sure this baby is healthy…

As if on cue, another contraction begins, reassuring me that all is well. I time the contraction, watching the second hand of the bathroom clock as it moves with precision from one number to the next, five seconds at a time. *Five, ten, fifteen, twenty, twenty-five, thirty…*

At last, the phone is ringing. Thank you, God. Thank you for listening! Thank you for answering my prayers. He's finally out of that meeting. He can come home and collect me. We can get in the car and go to hospital. No time to waste. Hello? Hello? Now I'm shouting. Are you there? Are you there? At first, there is no answer — just an exhausted breathing sound; a long, deep sigh. Then, in a calm, controlled voice, he tells me that he's coming home. He'll be here soon. And he's bringing help.

It was not the day for pretending. It was not the day for feigning excitement about my impending birth. No more smiles. No more fake laughter. I was there to do a job. I was there to give birth to my dead baby. I wasn't planning to say anything that first time, as we went up in the lift. I kept my head down, eyes focused on my fraying sandal straps. But nothing could hide my bulge from the well-meaning passenger in the navy blue suit. Nothing could stop her from politely inquiring about my baby. My baby is dead, I replied.

The hospital gave us a double room, with a spare bed for my husband. I hadn't realised we would be there overnight. It turned out to be two nights. My body didn't know what to do. It was confused. I needed three doses of synthetic hormone to get things started — two doses on Wednesday and one on Thursday morning. By Thursday afternoon, I was in labour. It was nothing like the movie trailer. Nothing like the videos in birth education classes. No excited anticipation; no sense of urgency; no raised voices; no commotion. Everything happened slowly, deliberately and clinically.

I had planned for a natural birth, without an epidural. But when the contractions became more intense, I couldn't see the point of enduring all that pain. I had read about the risks of epidurals, for both mother and baby, but none of that seemed to matter anymore. So what if the labour was a bit longer? So what if there was a greater risk of tearing? So what if they needed to use forceps? Who cared about a drop in fetal heart rate? My baby's heart wasn't even beating any more. I was physically trapped in that delivery suite for as long as it took to give birth, but mentally, I needed to be as far away as possible. Pain relief was a good start.

As well as blocking the pain, the epidural numbed my lower body, so I didn't physically feel the urge to push. I didn't feel it mentally either. I knew that once this baby was born, the nightmare of the past few days would become a tangible reality. I instinctively knew that my baby was dead, and the ultrasound had confirmed it, but a tiny part of me — the shocked, irrational part — kept hoping that we'd got it all wrong. That once my baby made it to the outside world, she would suddenly start breathing again. But of course, that was pure fantasy. Instead, my last push delivered a tiny, premature body that was slippery, crinkled and blue. And still. Very, very still.

I'm still trying to work out why he's 'bringing help.' All I need is him, and his car, to get me to hospital. Oh, God, what is he talking about? Perhaps he's rung for an ambulance? Maybe he's worried we won't get there in time? I guess I could be getting close. It's hard to tell really. I'm not sure how bad it's supposed to get.

I've finally managed to get out of the bath. I've timed it well, between contractions. I get dressed and check through my bag one more time: birth plan, bathrobe, nightgowns, slippers, socks, T-shirt, toiletries, glasses ... I'm interrupted by the sound of a key in the door. Thank you, God, he's home at last. But he's not alone. I hear voices — hushed voices, secret whispers, nervous muttering. He must be talking to the paramedics. The ambulance must be here. They're working out whether to stay here or go to hospital. I think hospital would be better. Hospital it is.

The morning after my stillbirth, a young woman from the funeral home visited the hospital to help us make arrangements. I think she was as new to the situation as we were. As she talked us through the options, she fidgeted awkwardly. We decided on a white infant casket with a pink and white floral spray. The service would be held at the crematorium chapel. The minister would choose the readings and the hymns. My husband and I would attend on our own. Our baby's ashes would be placed next to my father's, under the family memorial tree.

I wake up in hospital, expecting to see a bassinet at my bedside. It's not there. I glance down the bed and see the mound of my swollen belly under the covers. It's still there. My baby is still inside me. But there is no movement. I must be in between contractions. I look around the room and see my husband, slumped in a rocking chair in the far corner, asleep. He wakes with a start as the doctor enters the room.

I'm firing off questions but getting no answers. Neither of them will tell me what's going on. Their eyes are connected in a knowing look, as if they're keeping some dark secret. The doctor starts saying things that don't make sense. He says my morning sickness is real. My swollen breasts are real. My swollen belly is real. The sensations of fetal movement might feel very real. The only real difference is that there is no real baby and no real labour. The technical term is pseudocyesis, or phantom pregnancy.

I've stopped listening. He doesn't know what he's talking about. I can see my swollen belly; I can see my baby bump right in front of me. I can feel my baby moving again. Another contraction is about to start. Please, God, stay with me. Please, God, help me prove them wrong. Please, don't take this baby from me. You promised I could keep this one. Please, God, please.

I gaze intently at the clock on the wall. It's the size of a giant Frisbee, with huge black numbers marking the hours, and a long, delicate second hand counting the seconds, five at a time. I start timing the next contraction.

Five, ten, fifteen, twenty, twenty-five, thirty, thirty-five.

"Still Movement"

JOCELYN HOYLE is a journalist/sub-editor from Sydney, Australia. She's a self-confessed dag who loves walking, talking, and drinking (both wine and tea). She loves listening to all sorts of music — from Bach to The Beatles — and wishes her dance moves looked half as good as they felt. "Still Movement" is her first published story.

She says: "Stillbirth is one of those taboo topics that make people visibly squirm. I wanted to tell a story that might help explain its impact on parents. As a journo, I was jokingly advised to never let the facts get in the way of a good story. As a fiction writer, I love the freedom of being able to make up a story myself, with or without a few facts. To be honest, I wasn't sure how this story would go down, so I wrote it in secret, in fits and starts, and just hoped for the best."

Happily Ever After

PLEASE, GOD, let him telephone me now....

"Five hundred thousand, three hundred and sixty; five hundred thousand, three hundred and sixty-five; five hundred thousand, three hundred and seventy; five hundred thousand, three hundred and seventy-five —"

Nell's throat had gone sore long ago. Her lips were parched. Her tongue ached.

"Five hundred thousand, three hundred and eighty —"

At least her chair was comfortable. She'd heard that her predecessor had had to make do with a wooden seat, without a cushion.

"Five hundred thousand, three hundred and eighty-five —"

The phone sat atop a three-legged stool close enough to the wall so that the wire running to the socket wasn't taut. The phone itself rested in a cradle.

"Five hundred thousand, three hundred and ninety   "

The room was padded. Six by four, and bright white. There were no windows, and the seams of the door blended into the padding.

"Five hundred thousand, three hundred and ninety-five —"

The phone rang.

Nell's breath caught in her throat. She locked her muscles. A moment passed. The silence would have echoed off the walls, if it wasn't absorbed by them.

The phone trilled again. It shook in its cradle.

Nell let out her breath.

She curled her hands around the edges of the arms of her chair and pushed herself to her feet. She made it no further than a single step before she collapsed forward onto the floor. She landed next to the stool, her hand mere inches from one of the legs. The entire stool rattled as the phone continued to ring.

She ignored her bones' cracking as she raised herself onto her knees. She lifted the phone from its cradle.

The phone fell silent.

Nell brought the phone to her ear. "Hello?"

"Nell?"

Nell blinked. The voice was crackly and distant. A tear made its way down her cheek.

"This is she."

"Ha! Don't speak, just listen."

Nell gulped; some saliva trickled down her throat, and it soothed as much as it burned.

"This is Diana. I know you were expecting a man to ring. But he's not going to." The voice stopped, to be replaced by the sound of fabric moving across fabric.

Nell froze. Soft footfalls fell on the floor padding. A hand fell on her shoulder.

Nell gulped and turned. A woman was standing behind her, and beyond the woman the door was open.

Diana had a portable phone pressed to her ear. She hung it up; Nell's phone went dead.

Diana pocketed her phone and knelt by Nell's side. She still hadn't taken her hand off Nell's shoulder. Diana reached out with her free hand and grabbed Nell's phone; she pulled it from her grip and placed it back in its cradle.

"Let's get you out of here."

Diana stood and hooked her hands beneath Nell's

armpits. She pulled Nell to her feet and wrapped an arm around her waist. Nell sagged against her side, but Diana held her tight. She turned them both around.

Through the open door, there was nothing but white. It was as if stepping out of this room would have led into an ether: a nothingness. Nell whimpered and locked her muscles together.

"Come on," Diana grunted, and a swift nudge was all it took to get Nell moving.

In ten tentative steps, the two of them reached the door. Diana pulled Nell through.

The floor outside of the room was not padded. Nell screamed and sagged against Diana, who had to adjust her grip stop her from collapsing. She heaved Nell up onto her feet, and Nell cried out.

"I know it hurts," Diana said. "I know it does, baby. But it'll get better. I promise. Just don't scream any more, okay?"

Diana's adjusted grip made it easier for Nell to be dragged along, saving her from the effort of fighting to keep her feet moving in time with Diana's.

"You're doing great, babe," Diana said. "Just hang in there, okay?"

Nell hung her head as they continued to move.

"I know you might not remember me," Diana continued, "but I'm not asking you to, okay? All I'm asking is that you trust me."

Nell sniffed.

Diana continued pulling Nell along towards the end of the white corridor. She nearly fell when Diana shifted her grip on her. She gasped, but Diana caught her and apologised.

"I just need to get something from my pocket."

Nell watched Diana delve into her jeans pocket and pull out a white card with a strip of metallic silver running across its length. Diana touched the card to a black box on the wall:

a green light flashed, and a click sounded.

Diana stuffed the card back into her pocket and held Nell close to her again. "Okay, we're nearly there. You okay?"

Diana turned her face to Nell's, and Nell saw how wide her eyes were. There was something in Nell's throat, but it wasn't her voice. She just nodded and followed Diana's lead.

Diana opened the door in front of them. It gave way to another room, though this room was nothing like the room that Nell had been in for she couldn't remember how long: this room was black and lit only by artificial light coming from several screens around the room. Each screen had a dashboard set into a black column, and each black column had a seat in front of it, and each seat had someone in it, though none of them looked very alert and they were all rather limp.

"Don't look at that, babe," Diana said.

But Nell did look. It was hard to see with so little light, but she could make out blank, unseeing eyes set into heads resting upon necks that were not quite at the right angles, and fingers hanging limp from hands hanging limp from arms hanging limp from shoulders that were far too relaxed.

The screens in front of the people who were not paying attention showed rooms like the one Nell had been in: white padded rooms with chairs and stools and telephones and people dressed like Nell sitting in those chairs waiting for the telephones on the stools to ring. One of the screens showed a room with an empty chair.

Diana was still leading her forward, and forward was away from the bodies and the screens and the dashboards and the black columns. Nell looked forward to a part of the room that the light from the screens could barely reach.

Then the sound of heels clapping on the floor came from the darkness, and Diana stopped in her tracks.

A gun slipped out of the darkness, followed by a figure. The figure emerged from the feet up: from red heels to exposed shins to the hem of a black pencil skirt with a slit in the side to a white pinstriped blouse open just a little lower than was strictly necessary to a cruel smile on lips painted the same red as those shoes.

"I did wonder if we'd see you around here at some point, Miss Heath."

Diana bristled and tightened her grip on Nell. "And you wondered right. Give yourself a medal."

The woman chuckled, showing bright white teeth between those painted lips. "Well, you've had your fun now. It's time for Miss Thomas to get back to her room. And it looks like we'll be fitting you out for one now, Miss Heath. I think you've exhausted all the favours your father is owed."

Diana grit her teeth. "I'm not leaving without her."

"That's what I just said: you're not leaving. Maybe the judge will be lenient and put you in a room next to her. I doubt it, though. We don't want to encourage any … immoral behaviour."

Diana growled. Nell lowered her gaze to the floor, and just listened.

"Look around you, lady. You look at what I'm willing to do."

The woman hummed. There was a pause as she shifted, looking around the room. "You certainly have some talent. It's a shame your existence is illegal, we might have offered you a job."

Diana spat: a wad of saliva landed on the toe of the woman's shoe. The woman lifted her foot up on the heel and tutted.

"Such behaviour is unbecoming of a lady. Then again, so much of your behaviour is unbecoming of a lady."

"Shut up! I'm tired of being treated like this."

"And yet you're only saving one prisoner." The woman reached forward to Nell; Diana growled and stepped back, pulling Nell with her.

"Do *not* touch her."

The woman sighed and lowered her hand. "Miss Heath, you must see the asininity of your actions here today. Say you managed to escape with Miss Thomas. Say you made it to a hiding place. Say you two found a way to live out the rest of your abominable lives together. You've left so many here to their fates. All for the crime of not being loved by Diana Heath."

"I'll come back for the others."

The woman laughed. "I'm not sure I believe that. You only vowed yourself to Miss Thomas. 'Till death do us part'? I'm sure that could be arranged."

The woman flicked the safety off her gun. Diana yelped and yanked Nell in front of her: the woman's gun was pointed between Nell's eyes.

"Go on," Diana warned. "Shoot a prisoner. See where that gets you." The woman stood stock still for a moment.

What happened next was too fast for Nell to register.

The woman raised the gun above their heads and let off a shot. Diana grunted, and let go of Nell. Nell fell sideways onto her knees, then onto the floor. She caught herself on her arm and looked over in the direction of a second thud.

Diana was lying on the floor and blood was oozing from the back of her head.

Heels clopped over to Nell. The woman kneeled before Nell and put a hand on her shoulder. Nell could no longer see the gun.

"Miss Thomas?"

Nell turned away from Diana and looked at the woman. She had kind eyes, Nell realised, now that she could pay attention.

"Miss Thomas, you're okay now. That woman tried to kidnap you, but I stopped her. You can get back to your work now. Okay?"

A tear made its way down Nell's cheek.

"Now, now," the woman simpered, and rubbed her thumb over Nell's cheek. "None of that. It's over now. You don't need to be scared any more. Let's get you back to your room."

The woman disappeared into the darkness again, then reappeared pushing a wheelchair. She helped Nell up into it.

"There you go."

Nell sighed as she settled back into the wheelchair.

The woman wheeled Nell back down the corridor. The door to Nell's room was still open. The woman pushed her inside and put the phone back in its cradle. She held Nell under her arms to put her back in her own chair, then knelt in front of her.

"You've been so good, Miss Thomas," the woman smiled. "So very good, indeed. You've done exactly what we've asked of you, and never faltered even once."

She bit her lip.

"Unfortunately, Miss Heath has gone and ruined all of that for you now. She's deleted your progress. I'm very sorry to have to tell you this, but ... You'll have to start your task over again." She squeezed Nell's shoulder. "But you're so good at it, you'll have no problem catching up. You'll be there in no time. Okay?"

Nell blinked.

A moment passed.

Nell nodded.

"Excellent," the woman grinned. "It's just like before: wait for that phone to ring. Now, I'm going to leave you to it."

The woman smiled and stood up. She wheeled the chair back out of the room and closed the door behind her.

Nell settled back into her chair and opened her mouth. "Five; ten; fifteen; twenty; twenty-five; thirty; thirty-five...."

"Happily Ever After"

ELLEN GRACE is a student from London, England. She has been published in the *Bust-A-Rhyme Poetry Anthology*, *The Drabble*, and *Penny Shorts*.

She says: "This story, like so many of my stories, deals with my own experience of internalised homophobia and my anger towards it. More often than not, my characters are queer women facing homophobic regimes in dystopian futures, and usually they do not get to win against those regimes. Nell and Diana are unlucky in more ways than one, and unfortunately do not possess the power to overcome those who would deny them their existence. They cannot change the system, but they remain who they are."

God? Please.

"PLEASE. *GOD*? Let Him telephone me. Now the *devil?*— him I'd open the door for." Francis waited for his classmates to respond but got mostly studied stoniness. Facing Francis, Leo widened his eyes, then winced as Sister Dolores's leathery palm struck Francis's ear — really the whole side of his head — from behind.

"It's '*For him* I'd open the door.' And we'll see about that." She led Francis by his ringing ear toward the school building. Center door, where the office was. A sprightlier nun — one of those guitar-toting post-Vatican-II Sisters — could have hurt him more by walking faster, but lumbering Sister Dolores improvised, pulling his ear sideways every few steps or yanking down on it. In the office she pushed Francis onto the bench and proceeded into the back. "That boy cannot attend the field trip."

Francis couldn't hear the principal's response.

"I *insist*. Intolerable blasphemy. Intolerable." Sister Dolores emerged from the office. "Mrs. Allesandrini, call this boy's mother."

Mrs. A picked up the handset and spoke into it without dialing. "Sister, the boy we have out here is Francis Gilhooley." Mrs. A knew that Francis could not be sent home early because he walked his first-grade sister home. Francis again heard indistinguishable words from the office, then Mrs. A spoke into the phone again: "She can't, right? I mean…Yes, Sister." Mrs. A hung up and avoided Sister Dolores's withering, cloudy eyes.

The principal — no guitar, but modern enough to use her straight name which to this day Francis cannot remember — emerged. "Sister Dolores, may we confer? Mrs. Allesandrini, no need to make any calls. Mr. Gilhooley, I'll get to you soon enough. Stay there." The Sisters went into the office and closed the door. Mrs. A told Francis not to worry through a weak smile.

Sister Dolores emerged. With a twitchy scowl she directed Francis into the principal's office.

Francis explained. "Telephone or doorbell. It's just a game. Somebody names two people, and then somebody else has to say which one you'd want to call you and which you'd want at your front door. Plus you say why. Like, if somebody said St. Francis of Assisi or St. Francis Xavier, I'd pick St. Francis Assisi for the door because he might have puppies."

"Good choice. Xavier did most of his good work by talking, anyway. But, Mr. Gilhooley, do you expect me to believe that you boys were playing this game about saints?"

"No. No, Sister. The names could just as well be Nelson Rockefeller and Robert Kennedy."

"Hmm ... Or Evel Knievel and Captain Kangaroo?"

"I guess so."

"Or God and the Devil?"

Francis looked at the paperweight. "Yes, Sister. That was it."

"And who picked those two names?"

"One of the guys. I don't remember." (He knew it was Leo.) "I just answered, and that's what Sister Dolores heard."

"And who got the doorbell and who got the phone?"

"I don't remember that either." (He did.)

"Okay, Francis. This is no day to be talking about the devil. The bus is about to leave. Get back out there."

Francis was the last one on the bus, so he had to sit next

to Sister Ignatius right behind the driver. He had the window, which he looked out for the entire trip. The driver smelled like cigars and the Sister smelled like left-out cheese. Francis tried to open the window, but Sister scolded him for being a fussbudget. He could feel his classmates' mockery on his back. He knew Sister Dolores was behind the bus in the station wagon with the other Sisters. She'd be at the shrine.

On the bus, Sister Ignatius or another Sister walked up and down the aisle, brow-furrowing and swatting as necessary. A few CCD kids from public school were on the trip, and they got the most skeptical attention. This was unnecessary because those kids were more intimidated by Sisters than Francis and his classmates.

Francis was scrupulously well-behaved at the shrine. He sat quietly through the filmstrip about Father Isaac Jogues, who got himself martyred in 1650-something trying to save the souls of ungrateful savages. But Francis would remember nothing; he fixated on the punishment awaiting him at school. Sure, some Sisters looked kindly on his cheerful devotion to walking his sister home, but he was not untouchable. He stayed in line during the tour and contemplated the longhouse dioramas for a duration he reckoned any Sister would deem respectful.

He was briefly distracted from his misery. The children — the Sisters referred to everyone as *the children* even though some of the boys had lip fuzz and the girls were developing, and Francis sometimes wondered if they found it as patronizing as he did...

The children were marched along an indirect route from the museum toward a building with a makeshift lunchroom, which route passed the year-round Christmas Creche, around which the children were instructed to gather. Francis put himself near the front and pursed his lips; it would be impertinent for a boy to be seen smiling on the very morning he was heard boasting about opening the door to Satan. A shrine volunteer, a girl just younger than Francis's college brother, related trivia about the sculptor whose piety and the parish whose generosity had together established the statuary. Behind the crowd, Sister Maria Crescentia and Sister Teresa of Avila argued toe-to-toe, hissing without regard for the children, none of whom had ever contemplated such a breach of protocol. The children began to turn around and gawk.

Francis, whose attentiveness was feigned, never noticed the tour guide's increasingly false timbre. He turned around only after the guide stopped talking altogether and craned her neck toward the bickering Sisters.

The argument had been a long time coming. Before arriving to teach social studies, Sister Teresa had spent years ministering to *American Indians* in Minnesota and the Dakotas, where she was in the vanguard of the linguistic change to *Native Americans*. Now in her first year of teaching, she would spend too much classroom time discussing the plight of the Native Americans and not enough time on the standard curriculum, a decision for which she would eventually be reprimanded when the administrators finally caught on. At the shrine, she had found the filmstrip belittling to the Native-American experience.

The argument had crescendo'd without Francis's attention and was now in full flower. Sister Teresa said "I'm not sure, Sister Maria, that I understand your reluctance. It would just be a few moments during the lunch prayers."

"I'm sure the lunch prayers offered by the chaplain will be ideally suited to the day," said Sister Maria, "...without supplemental digressions."

"But Sister Maria, the children would benefit from another viewpoint."

"When you've been here for more than a few months, Sister Teresa, you'll be equally sure that the children have too many viewpoints as it is. Thank you, Sister Teresa. That will be all."

Sister Teresa ignored the invocation of rank. "Sister

Maria, my experience elsewhere prevented me from being here with you, where my opinions might have more conveniently indurated. We can both look forward to that in the coming years. But until then, perhaps the children would benefit from another" — she almost said *viewpoint* — "perspective."

"Please. Perspective? That's enough, Sister." Sister Maria stressed *enough* exactly as she would when threatening an unruly class. Standing on the path with their backs to the creche, the students were enthralled by clerical fissure.

Even Sister Teresa, who'd met Sister Maria only weeks earlier, recognized the tone and took offense. She turned her back theatrically, but Sister Maria continued. "We all know you have a tomahawk to grind." She pantomimed a tomahawk chop. But Sister Teresa had spun away so vigorously that the chop caught the billowing fabric of Sister Teresa's veil. Sister Maria, finding the fabric at her fingertips, grabbed it reflexively. Sister Teresa, hearing the offensive reference, extended her planned 180 into a 360 so she could further illuminate things to Sister Maria.

And that's how it happened. Sister Teresa continued to spin, fast, while Sister Maria held Teresa's veil. It was torn from Teresa's head, dislodging her spectacles so roughly that a cut was opened on the bridge of her nose. The spectacles fell to the ground. The tour guide ran to the lunchroom to fetch up the other Sisters who were setting up the tables and folding chairs.

After the tour guide ran away, two enterprising boys stepped into the creche to rearrange the figures into something scandalous. They could move only the smaller statues. They did their best to make a shepherd cornhole a calf. The choreography was unconvincing, so they looked for a rock to prop up the calf's backside.

Arriving at the lunchroom, the breathless tour guide could only manage "Now. At the creche. Something happened. Now."

Down the hill, Sister Teresa was on her hands and knees, looking for her spectacles and shouting at Sister Maria. She used the harshest words she could muster: uninformed, uncharitable, even un-Christian. Silently holding Teresa's headgear, Sister Maria looked disoriented but neither guilty nor contrite.

The boys in the creche found a rock and were ferrying it together toward the calf.

At that moment, the chaplain Father Ossifa was sprinting down the hill shouting "Hey-yay-yay-yay," one syllable per footfall. The boys in the creche heard him and tried to escape. One boy dropped his half of the rock and the other boy fell awkwardly, headbutting the donkey as the rock fractured its forelimbs. The donkey tipped over and smashed. The priest ran straight to the creche and clotheslined the upright boy who was trying to scoot back into the crowd. The other boy was lying in donkey shards bleeding from his forehead.

"Stand up. Get over here. What is your name?" Father held the upright boy by the collar while waiting for a response from the other, who got up, holding one hand to his forehead and using the other to brush donkey dust from his shirt.

Sister Maria reached the front of the creche. "One of these boys," she waved her hand still holding Sister Teresa's veil, "is from the public school." Francis knew this to be false. The boy Sister Maria didn't recognize was a recent transfer from another school. Leo caught Francis's eye as if to say *He's one of us, or we'll take him if he lives through the day.* Francis did not feel the kinship that Leo felt for the new boy.

Others arrived from the lunch room. The tour guide led Sister Angelica to Sister Teresa, who was standing, holding her glasses, and dabbing at the cut on her nose. Leo dragged Francis partway up the hill (by the elbow, not the ear) toward the lunchroom, so they could take in both dramas.

About this time, Francis's mother was in the emergency room watching doctors fail to revive Francis's younger sister from the asthma attack she suffered that morning in class, induced by a show-and-tell rabbit. Mrs. Gilhooley crumbled. "Please, God, do not do this to her. To us — anyone — me — not her. Not her. *Me*."

The doctors said the obligatory things to her and a nurse touched the back of her neck. The hospital chaplain arrived — a priest who lived in the rectory of the Gilhooley's parish and occasionally said Mass there. The medical personnel left. The priest took up a position on one side of the gurney; Mrs. Gilhooley was on the other. Although the medical consensus held that Colleen has stepped fully through death's door, the chaplain administered extreme unction, retroactively. This was improper.

Sacraments can be administered only to the living. On the other hand, the church knows that the moment of death cannot be pinpointed, so in ambiguous cases, priests are allowed to prefix the prayers with "If thou art alive," enclosing the entire rite in a conditional. But the priest mercifully omitted these words, not wishing to stir false hope in Mrs. Gilhooley, or perhaps wishing to reassure her that God would not disqualify the blessing on a technicality. He put away his equipment and stepped back from the gurney. He spoke the way priests do about death, as a teachable moment about what happens to the soul when God calls it home. Mrs. Gilhooley heard the words, but let them wash over her without interpretation. Eventually he turned to more practical matters and she began to parse.

"The hospital has staff to take care of things from here. Just choose a funeral home and we will work directly with them to get her — to handle all those matters. Shall I drive you home? School will let out soon."

"No," she said. "Take me to the school so I can get to Francis. Is that okay? I know you offered to take me home and I'm requesting more. Forgive me for that. Perhaps you have other duties here." At this last she wept briefly. "I want to get to Francis. The older kids can find their way home from high school as usual. Wait. Agnes has a rehearsal. I guess I do want them to come home straightaway. Should she go to rehearsal? What do people do in these situations?"

"It is no problem. I will drive you to the school to pick up Francis. We can decide how to tell your other children on the way. Then we'll call the high school from the grammar school office, if you want that. Alright, Mary? Stay here while I run upstairs to fetch the car keys."

Mrs. Gilhooley waited and wondered: What kind of life must it be to carry your last rites kit on your person, but not your car keys?

In the lunchroom at the shrine, the Sisters huddled with Father Ossifa, contemplating whether to cancel the afternoon program and return to school immediately. Sister Dolores lobbied indignantly for immediate cancellation of the program and for sending the children back to school without lunch. "Their hunger shall be an offering," she said.

Father Ossifa was sympathetic to her without agreeing. "Sister," said the chaplain, "I am as outraged as you are. Perhaps more so as I was always fond of the donkey. But allowing the innocent children to eat lunch will give the boys who defiled the creche some time to remove the donkey pieces before the Auxiliary Bishop arrives."

Sister Angelica stiffened. "God save us, *the Bishop*." A part of the afternoon program — it was to be a surprise for the children — was the appearance of the Bishop, who had agreed to stop at the shrine while driving back from high services in a western outpost of the archdiocese. "If he diverts himself to see us, we cannot be elsewhere."

"Those children," said Sister Dolores, "do not deserve an audience with the Bishop. What would he say about such barbarism?"

"Indeed, Sister," said the chaplain. "But we will not mention it. The guilty boys and I will remove the remains of the donkey while the other children eat lunch. We do not want those children meeting the Bishop on empty stomachs."

"Fine," sneered Sister Dolores. "For the Bishop's benefit, the unimplicated children will get lunch. But those boys who invaded the creche; they must be taken away."

The chaplain smiled and turned to Sister Maria, whose face had stopped bleeding and whose glasses were once again situated properly. "Can you drive?"

The unimplicated children ate in enforced silence. Down the hill, the chaplain helped the boys wheelbarrow the donkey to a hiding spot behind a shed. They raked over the ground where the donkey had stood. Then Sister Maria drove the guilty boys back to school, where they sat on the office bench waiting for the principal to emerge and punish them. The principal's door was closed because inside, she sat with Mrs. Gilhooley and the hospital chaplain, serving tea and reminding Mrs. Gilhooley that Francis was at the shrine with his classmates. They made some calls to the high school.

After lunch, Francis and his classmates continued their tour of the grounds until the Bishop arrived. Then they trundled back into the lunchroom where he spoke briefly about the merits of studiousness: *Not only will it help some of you grow up to be doctors and lawyers, but some of you might soon be called to the cloth, and a contemplative frame of mind will buttress that career too.* He blessed them all and left in his Buick. The remainder of the day transpired without incident. Everyone kept their head down.

When it was time to return home, a logistical issue arose. The station wagon, which was actually a decommissioned airport limousine with four bench seats and room for eleven Sisters (or a driver plus 14 children), had returned to school with only Sister Maria and the two miscreants. The bus would have to accommodate two fewer students and nine more Sisters. Sister Ignatius — the one Francis has sat with on the morning bus ride — called the school to see if the

station wagon could be sent back. She was told that
everyone was to return without delay.

Students were instructed to sort themselves by height,
with the tallest boarding first and proceeding all the way to
the back. For the front portion of the bus, each pair of seats
on the right side would accommodate three small girls and
each pair on the left would have one student and one Sister.
Francis again found himself behind the driver, this time
sharing a seat with a less intimidating Sister. He was not
commanded into the seat; but welcomed. He relaxed,
believing that he was out of trouble, that his indiscretion
would not get much attention from the school's punitive
apparatus that would be focused on graver misdeeds. His
stomach settled. He looked forward to being home as he
listened to Sister Angelica walk down the aisle, passing along
the rows and tallying the headcount: "Five, ten, fifteen,
twenty, twenty-five, thirty, thirty-five…."

"God? Please."

JOSEPH MAGUIRE is a computer scientist from New England, in the United States. "God? Please." is his first published story.

He says: "Although I am the product of more than a decade of Catholic education, this is a work of fiction. All characters except 17th Century missionary Isaac Jogues are concocted; although, like Francis, I did spend a lot of childhood energy speculating inaccurately about what was happening around me. Another thing: Both Francis and I retain into adulthood the names of all our dyspeptic Sisters, but forget the names of the pleasant ones. Unfair."

Hayleigh Clarkson

Rue de Dubois

"PLEASE, GOD, let him telephone me now." Maria was in her front living room pacing back and forth in front of the large bay windows. She was dressed in a long dark coat, black hat and a pair of men's shoes with worn-out soles she had found lying in the gutter. Her suitcase, a small brown one with a crumbling and peeling exterior that once belonged to her papa sat at the back door ready for her escape.

She didn't have long. The gun shots were echoing up the street towards her, and children's screams filled the air. She peered out from behind the heavy blind. The street was still in forced blackout. All she could see were the pinprick head lights of the police van carrying her Jewish friends. She looked across the road at the Wasserman's house and saw them climbing over their fence and disappearing into the night.

Maria looked down at her arm and traced the faint outline of the star she was forced to stitch in. When she joined the Six Daisies she'd cut the threads loose, risking not only her life but those of her family and friends.

She was running out of time. The French police were moving closer, picking off their targets one by one. They were warned that the police were to raid their neighbourhood. The Red Orchestra had filtered information to her through their intricate resistance network and she had passed the facts down the line of the street. But she didn't think it would happen so soon.

Maria moved away from the window and back to the stairs. She sat down next to the wooden desk that she used to do her homework on. In a sliver of moonlight that broke through from a tear in the heavy blind, she could make out her name she had scratched into the desk many years earlier. But now it was just her.

She didn't know what had happened to her family. She had gone out at night to transport an infant to a safe house a few streets over, and when she returned the door was kicked in and they were gone. Neighbours said they heard a lot of shouting and gun shots, but were too afraid to venture outside to watch. She could only assume that like other Jewish families in her neighbourhood, they were transported to a concentration camp.

The police were only a few doors down. She could hear them yelling at the occupants to get out of their house. There was banging and the pleading sounds of mothers being forcibly torn from their children. Windows were being smashed. She could hear the shards of glass tinkling down onto the footpath. A slew of gunshots cut through the air and then silence.

Suddenly the phone rang.

Maria quickly grabbed the receiver and gave her all clear code. She waited for the familiar voice to deliver the instructions.

"Infant. Boy. 55 Rue de Dubois."

She slammed the receiver back down, ran to the back door, grabbed her suitcase and left.

Outside the air was bitterly cold. She could see her breath in front of her as she ran across the back yard and pushed aside the hidden plank in the fence. It swung away, leaving her enough room to slip through and into the neighbouring yard of Madame Laurent.

She'd known Madame Laurent for many years. It was he who got her involved with the Six Daisies. Madame Laurent was one of the six founders of the resistance group created to save the lives of Jewish children. When the Gestapo first started deporting Jews to the camps, they never took children. They were too young to be of use to them. But as the war grew more violent, so did the Gestapo. They started deporting anyone who was Jewish, regardless of age. Children as young as three were being ripped from their families and thrown into concentration camps. They didn't survive alone for long, and if they did, they were taken to the gas chambers and slaughtered.

Maria sunk to the ground and crawled around the grass, feeling her way forward until she found a small rock. She pulled on the rock and up came a large hidden door. A loud crash behind her tore her attention away from the shelter. She could see between the gaps in the fence the police swarming her house. Quickly she threw her suitcase down the stairs, shuffled her petite body inside and closed the door. Above her, she could hear the muffled footsteps of the police raiding her back yard. She could hear their dark voices but couldn't make out what they were saying. Maria stayed still, not willing to move in case they could hear her. Gradually, the officers moved away and onto the next property.

She let out a breath she didn't know she was holding. Down in the shelter, Madame Laurent was getting the candles ready.

"How are you dear?"

"Honestly? Scared. I got out just in time. I have a child to collect tomorrow night, too."

"Is that a good idea? The police will be roaming the streets looking for escapees."

"Do I have a choice? He needs my help."

She cocked her head at Maria and sighed.

"Come and take a seat, dear."

Maria and Madame Laurent sat in chairs opposite each other, sipping on cups of cold water and nibbling on stale crackers. They whispered to each other, sharing stories of their families and their lives before the war before gently drifting off to sleep.

Midway through the night, an air raid siren started squealing and jolted them awake. Footsteps were thundering above their heads as people ran to find shelter. They would be safe when the bombs started falling, but still Maria and Madame Laurent huddled in the corner together with their heads down and their warm hands clinging to each other in a silent prayer. The ground began to shudder as bomb after bomb destroyed their picturesque town. Dust floated down on to their heads like snow, creating a gentle grey coat. Ceramic mugs that sat on a wooden shelf crashed to the floor.

When the bombs stopped, the world became eerily silent and they drifted back into a restless slumber.

In the morning, the birds were back to chirping and a slither of sunlight bathed the stairs in a golden glow. Maria stuck her head out of the shelter and was immediately engulfed by smoke and the smell of burning timber. She crawled out of the shelter and stood up. Flames were licking her upstairs bedroom window. The lower half of the house was a blackened mess of rubble. Maria collapsed to the ground and cried. Big gulping sobs of loss convulsed out of her. Everything she owned. *Gone*. Memories. *Gone*. The little bear with a missing eye that belonged to her *petite sœur*. Her papa's books and papers from his research into wildlife that would help the government set up sanctuaries for birds close to extinction. Her maman's beautiful pearls, her cookbooks, her precious notes that she left in her school lunch. *All gone*.

Madame Laurent moved in beside her and knelt down. She wrapped her arms around her.

"Don't worry, my dear," she said, "we will get back at them. Mark my words. We will get our revenge."

The two women spent their day helping displaced Jewish neighbours find safer accommodation for the following night. Madame Laurent was right, the police were still wandering around the neighbourhood searching for any leftovers. Just after lunch, they knocked on her door. Madame Laurent ordered Maria to hide out the back.

"Move!" the officer yelled when he stormed through her front door and into the sitting room.

"Where is she?" he asked, flicking his eyes over her family treasures, no doubt searching for items he could loot once she was thrown out.

"I don't know who you are talking about, sir."

"The girl next door. You've been helping her."

"Are you talking about young Maria? *Oui*, I have been delivering her cooked dinners on the odd night. And I think I knitted her a scarf last winter … or was that her *petite sœur*? I forget now. Forgive an old woman her forgetful mind."

The officer studied her, then relaxed.

"Have you seen her?"

"Not for a few days, sir. I believe she left to stay with family in America. Well, that was what Suzette told me. Not that we can take her at face value. Her husband was a terrible —"

"Enough!" the officer cut in.

He walked towards the door and turned.

"When you see her, tell her we are looking for her. And we will find her."

"*Oui*, Sir."

Madame Laurent darted to her front window and watched the officer march across the street and knock on another door. She knew they'd be back. But she didn't know when.

Later that night as the sun set and the streets dissolved into their inky darkness, Maria left the house to collect her child. She dressed in her dark coat with black hat, and Madame Laurent loaned her proper shoes that fit better than the ones she had found.

The night was not as cold as the one before. She shoved her hands in her pockets and felt for the papers that would protect her from interrogation. Maria darted across the street and down a *cul-de-sac*, following the same path the Wasserman's had taken the night prior. She walked along quietly, keeping close to the houses and into the shadows cast by the moon. She weaved herself around the barriers and down a lane nudged in between two houses. Both were empty, windows broken and their belongings strewn across the yard. Her eyes began to adjust to her surroundings. Ahead she could see a dark mass on the ground. A body.

Maria stopped and looked around. The place was silent. She inched closer to the body and let out a cry. It was Madame Wasserman. Her body was riddled with bullet holes. Her blood had spilled out, staining the ground she lay on. The stench was the worst. Her bare feet were ghostly pale and sat absorbing her own blood. But there was nothing Maria could do. She knelt next to her and gently closed her eyelids. She said a silent prayer then continued on.

It wasn't long before she came across a group of officers raiding a house. The owner, a lonely Jewish man, stood outside his property and watched them loot whatever they thought was worth money. He was wearing filthy pants and a thin coat with a yellow star stitched into the sleeve. They had torn down the blackout blinds. His sitting room was brightly lit by candles and Maria could see the officers tearing their way through his drawers, throwing photo frames and china to the floor. She kept to the shadows and snuck by quietly, but the old man sensed her there and turned. He was crying. She whispered to him, "Don't worry. We will get back at them. Mark my words. We will get our revenge."

He nodded his understanding and went back to watching his life's possessions being destroyed.

Maria made it to the house. 55 Rue de Dubois. She walked up the stone steps and knocked on the door. The door creaked open and a voice hissed at her to get inside. She went into the hall and stood silently. The room was filled with dark mahogany furniture. She could smell dust and body odour. On the walls were photos of a family who had long abandoned their home, leaving it in the hands of the Six Daisies.

"*Mademoiselle*," a voice said gently, "this is Henri."

A little Jewish boy peered out from behind the woman's skirt. His eyes were wide with fear and he clutched a ragged bear close to his chest. He reminded Maria of her *petite sœur*. The fear she saw in her when the first bombs started to drop. Maria bent down to his height.

"*Bonjour, Monsieur Henri. Je suis Maria,*" she said softly, "I'm going to take you to a safe house to live."

"Do you know where my mummy is?" he whispered.

"Oh. No, sweetheart," she replied, looking up at the woman, "but I'm sure she is safe and well."

He nodded back at her. Maria held out her hand and he moved towards her, closing his little damp palm in hers.

"Come on, Henri. Let's go for an adventure," she smiled down at him.

"Look after him, Maria. This little boy is very special."

Maria looked back at her and said with every ounce of her being that she would protect him, no matter what.

Maria and Henri left the house and she guided him back the way she came. They walked slowly together, his little feet scuffing the ground and his teddy swinging at his side.

"What is your bear's name?" Maria asked.

Henri didn't reply. He kept his head down, swinging his bear back and forth in time to his steps. She squeezed his hand gently to let him know she was someone he could trust. He squeezed back.

They were approaching the house Maria saw raided only an hour ago. She could see a pink haze in the sky and knew immediately what it meant. As they neared, the scent of smoke grew stronger. She could hear the snapping and crackling of the flame eating its way through the timber.

They rounded the corner and there it was, a giant inferno of multiple houses burning to the ground. Maria looked around for the owners but the street was empty.

"Where are all the people?" asked Henri.

"I don't know, sweetheart."

They kept walking, keeping their distance from the flames, then Maria suddenly stopped. "Henri, close your eyes," she ordered.

"Why?"

"Because I said so."

Maria guided Henri around a row of trees lining a neighbouring field. Swaying from the trees were the occupants of the houses. Their bodies stripped of all their clothing. Their hands tied behind their backs. Amongst the shadows of the trees, they looked like they were floating. She said a silent prayer for them and moved on. When the bodies were out of sight, she let Henri open his eyes.

The sounds of the fire were fading into the distance when they reached the lane where Madame Wasserman lay. Maria scanned the path ahead of her but the mass was gone. Her heart started to race. Someone had been there. The only people to move the body would have been the police.

They walked down the lane quietly, and at the end Maria stopped. She could see a dark van outside Madame Laurent's house. She moved Henri in behind a bush and watched the police escorting Madame Laurent away. Her hands were tied behind her back. An officer had a gun pointed at her head.

Maria crouched down next to Henri. Her gloved hand was covering her mouth.

Madame Laurent stopped at the base of her steps. She raised her head and took a deep breath.

Maria's eyes started filling with tears. She'd never had a chance to say thank you. Or goodbye.

Madame Laurent's voice filled the night. She proudly

cried, "Mark my words! We will get our revenge!"

Her voice was still echoing when a gun shot rang out.

Henri screamed.

Madame Laurent fell forward onto the pavement.

The officers looked towards them and Maria whispered, "Stay still."

It was too late. An officer started walking their way.

Maria grabbed Henri's hand and dragged him back down the path. She forced him under a wire fence and followed, snagging her hat on the sharp prongs.

She dragged him over the broken pieces of furniture and into an empty house. Maria desperately looked around for a place to hide. Did she go upstairs and risk cornering themselves? Or hide in the storage closet?

She went to walk through the door into the kitchen when she heard a creak on the other side. She froze. Gently she removed her hand from the door handle and retreated back into the room.

She noticed the floor boards had been removed at the base of the stairs. She whispered to Henri to stay quiet, and motioned for him to wiggle down the hole and under the floorboards. He went in first and Maria followed, snaking down on her stomach and onto the dirt ground.

The officer entered the room. He stopped on top of them, smoking a cigarette and flicking the ash down onto her coat. She covered her mouth with her hand and got Henri to do the same. They lay still. When the officer moved upstairs, she whispered quietly to Henri.

"Are you okay, sweetheart?"

"*Oui, Madame.*"

"Good. So, Henri, do you go to school?" Henri nodded.

She was trying to distract him, to take his mind off the situation. But she was also trying to distract herself. She didn't know if either of them would make it out alive.

"Are you good at counting?"

"*Oui, Madame.*'

"Can you count in fives?"

"I think so."

"Okay. Let's count together."

With an officer upstairs searching for them, Maria and Henri lay side-by-side whispering to each other and manipulating Henri's bear to dance.

"Five, ten, fifteen, twenty, twenty-five, thirty, thirty-five…."

"Rue de Dubois"

HAYLEIGH CLARKSON is a support officer with the Hamilton police in New Zealand. She holds a BA in English Literature and Gender Studies, and has been writing since she was a little girl. "Rue de Dubois" is her first published story.

She says: "I've always adored historical fiction, and when I discovered that women in France helped to save Jewish children, I knew it was a story I had to tell. I wrote the story during downtime at work and sent it round all my co-workers for feedback. They loved it so much that it has now become a novel!"

Max Stanton

A Game of Telephone

Please God let him telephone me **now**
Please God let him telephone me **ten**
Please God let him telephone me **fifteen**
Please God let him telephone me **twenty**
Please God let him telephone me **twenty-five**
Please God let him telephone me **thirty**
Please God let him telephone me **thirty-five**

Please God let him telephone **me** now
Please God let him telephone **my name** ten
Please God let him telephone **namely** fifteen
Please God let him telephone **in other words** twenty
Please God let him telephone **i.e.** twenty-five
Please God let him telephone **1E** thirty
Please God let him telephone **thirty** thirty-five

Please God let him **telephone** me now
Please God let him **communicate** my name ten
Please God let him **séance** namely fifteen
Please God let him **ghost** in other words twenty
Please God let him **apparition** i.e. twenty-five
Please God let him **vision** 1E thirty
Please God let him telephone thirty thirty-five

Please God let **him** telephone me now
Please God let **man** communicate my name ten
Please God let **woman** séance namely fifteen
Please God let **child** ghost in other words twenty
Please God let **good** apparition i.e. twenty-five
Please God let **decent vision** 1E thirty
Please God let **twenty twenty-five** thirty thirty-five

Please God **let** him telephone me now
Please God **permit** man communicate my name ten
Please God **allow** woman séance namely fifteen
Please God **forbid** child ghost in other words twenty
Please God **rebel** good apparition i.e. twenty-five
Please God **teenage** decent vision 1E thirty
Please God **fifteen** twenty twenty-five thirty thirty-five

Please **God** let him telephone me now
Please **creator** permit man communicate my name ten
Please **messenger** allow woman séance namely fifteen
Please **prophet** forbid child ghost in other words twenty
Please **Moses** rebel good apparition i.e. twenty-five
Please **commandments** teenage decent vision 1E thirty
Please **ten** fifteen twenty twenty-five thirty thirty-five

Please God let him telephone me now
Pleasure creator permit man communicate my name ten
Contentment messenger allow woman séance namely fifteen
Satisfaction prophet forbid child ghost in other words twenty
Victory Moses rebel good apparition i.e. twenty-five
V commandments teenage decent vision 1E thirty
Five ten fifteen twenty twenty-five thirty thirty-five

"A Game of Telephone"

MAX STANTON is a retired semiotician from Rhode Island, in the United States. "A Game of Telephone" is his first published story.

He says: "I saw the first line and I saw the last line and the number 7 jumped out at me. Exactly seven words in each. So not just a prime number, but a double Mersenne prime. I thought about the 7 Stages of Man (from 'As You Like It') and the number of notes in the diatonic scale (ABCDEFG); but it was the seven days of Creation in Genesis (2:2-3) that clinched it. I immediately knew I wanted to perform a literal re-Creation, a text-based morphing from first line to last, word by word. That's how I would chart a path from Parker's opening to closing lines. I wrote several short programs in R, using a public domain dictionary and word nets, but in the end I fell back to Google Search to generate a simple Bayesian network to trace each semantic path. OK, more conceptual art than heartfelt poetry, but I was pleased with how it turned out."

A Promise

PLEASE, GOD, let him telephone me now.

I wasn't supposed to be here. No one should be here, on this roof, in this weather.

Why hadn't he called yet? The instructions had been clear.

I watched the rain form shapes on the window panes of the apartment across the street. They merged together like magnetic rivers. They dripped down and formed pools on the window sill which flowed over the edge, quickly turning into torrents eaten by the drain. I imagined I was one, just a drop of water, washed away, clean.

I curled my hands in tight against my palms, grasping hopelessly for warmth.

Surely he would call soon.

From my high vantage point I watched a middle-aged woman chase a small boy around their living room. It was bedtime but like all children he probably found the storm too exciting to sleep through. Had I not been in the middle of it I might have found sympathy with him.

The howling wind plastered dark, wet, locks against my cheeks. I fingered the match-box sized phone in my pocket. Maybe soon?

I checked the hour. Quarter to nine. The boy in apartment 303 hid behind the couch where perhaps he thought his mother couldn't see. She returned to their well-lit living room, sat down, and threw up her hands as if she'd given up. But I knew she hadn't. She was just pretending.

Like the last several nights. It's something all good parents do from time to time. Perhaps if mine had been more like that I wouldn't be where I was now.

Their window shone in the darkness, like a candle in an empty church. For the briefest of moments I pretended I was there, warm and loved.

Why hadn't he called yet?

How nice it must be to have a family. The boy was quickly found, or had he given up? Too easy kid, I would have stuck it out longer. It would be a while before she got him to bed though. It always was.

I couldn't feel my fingers anymore but that was okay. It was almost over. Only a few more minutes. He had time, just enough time. Surely he would call.

The wind beat at my face. The mother finally got the boy to sleep, or so it seemed. He would be back awake and wandering soon. He always was. Up and running around until well past nine-twenty every night for the last week, and probably the weeks before that. He was always causing trouble for his parents, but tonight was different.

Tonight his dad wasn't here. Where was he?

Thunder clapped. The apartment lights suddenly turned back on. The mother had a book. Perhaps she thought reading would help soothe her son to sleep. They curled up on the couch for all the heavens to see, loved by someone who wasn't there. Somewhere in the distance a cat yowled. But no phone rang.

Where was he?

I raised the rifle, and lined the sights up through the window of apartment 303. He had forty seconds left to call.

Five, ten, fifteen, twenty.

Twenty-five, thirty, thirty-five.

"A Promise"

ASHLEY STEWART is a PhD student in engineering from Christchurch, New Zealand. She's a climber, canyoneer, and wine taster, whose main hobby is collecting new hobbies. "A Promise" is her first published story.

She says: "Count-ups and countdowns always inspire tense moments. That, combined with waiting for a telephone call, suddenly put me in the head of someone on a roof in the rain with a rifle. Why are they waiting and who they are waiting for? Are they a blackmailer, waiting to hear about a payment from their mark? Or a spurned lover out for revenge, hoping their lost love will call them off at the last minute? Maybe they're a time-traveler with a deadline to kill young Hitler and they're hoping to hear that the transporter can get them safely back to the future? Or maybe it's something else entirely. I like to ask questions and let the reader wonder. I like to let myself wonder, too."

Counting Inches in the Emergency Room

PLEASE, GOD, let him telephone me now. You think this out loud as you sit on the toilet in the unisex bathroom at the emergency room. The urologist you saw said test results can take anywhere from ten minutes to four hours, it just depended on how much the lab was backed up.

Ten minutes felt like four hours.

The PA system drowns out your groans of pain.

You have to pee, but you can't. You should know the size of the kidney stone by now, if indeed that's what it is. You should know what you're dealing with, but your doctor still hasn't called back. It's impossible to think that something smaller than a pebble along the lake shore outside your mother's cabin could cause so much pain. But it does.

This isn't your first stone. You know what you're up against. You've had enough of red toilet bowls. You're ready to pass this. In a way, the pain that strikes you is relieving. You can see the finish line.

The hot knife in your kidney twists. You have to stand up, to rub away the pain and scream at God for allowing this to happen to you. Have you really done anything so bad to deserve this?

Your mother would tell you it was all part of God's plan for you. Or to stop drinking so much black tea.

A red mist splatters out of you like hairspray from a

bottle. Most of it dissipates in the air. Some paints the toilet. You never had to pee worse in your life than in this moment. There is no relief because, as you look down, you see that your urethra is blocked.

It isn't a kidney stone, you think. Oh, God, it isn't a kidney stone.

What *is* that?

A three-inch strand like a noodle of cooked spaghetti dangles out of your urethra. You think it is a blood clot. You've heard of this.

The strand begins to squirm.

You pull back as though to draw away from it. You tense your muscles and rise up on your toes. It reels back like a fishing line into your body, slowly.

"*Shit.*"

You can't let this happen. You have no choice but to pinch the tip of it and hold it there until you can catch your breath.

It wriggles like the worms you and your sister used to harvest after spring rainstorms. It is neither slimy nor ridged like worms of the earth. It is smooth like the tubes it slithers through. It is red and pulses with warmth and life.

You could pull it out, like the earthworms that tried to get away from your fingers as a child.

Sometimes, though, they would break.

You pull. It resists and tries to reel inside of you. You pull harder.

A hot poker of pain travels up through your urethra to some place deep inside of you, some organ you've never felt before. It is like someone tugging a barbed catheter out of you. Your eyes burn from this. A wave of black rolls over them. You sway. Your knees tremble and want to give up. Maybe you should give up. Maybe you should let it go and pretend this never happened to you. This was someone else's experience or a really bad dream, because dealing with a kidney stone is insanity.

Catheters remind you of your mother, too. You couldn't stand the smell of the plastic bags they came in. It made you sick. It made you realize there was no way around what you had to do. Your siblings would understand if you told them. None of them even wanted the cabin after she died. None of them spoke to her. They had left you alone to deal with her. They didn't deserve an explanation.

Your mother never liked the worms. They were filthy, she said. They carried diseases. They could get inside of you.

You look to your phone on the counter by the sink, but it is a useless shingle of metal and glass. You think to cry out to the other ER-goers, but then the worm retracts.

You can't bear to pull it out further, but you hold it there, pinched between your thumb and finger. Bamboo shoots of pain ramrod your urethra. The pain brings you to your knees, but it also brings everything into focus. Especially the toilet paper holder.

You yank out the rod.

You black out for a moment, quick, like a light switched off and back on. You catch yourself before you bang your head against the back of the toilet. Tears wet your eyes and slither down the bridge of your nose.

You scream for it to get out of you.

It is retracting, but you catch it in time. You lose some progress.

When you pull, the pain is different, worse somehow. You get sick. Twice.

The pain has numbed most of your body, but you were never one to quit. You remember how much strength it took to hold down that pillow. You never expected her to fight back. Your arms trembled and burned then as they do now. The rest of your body was ice.

You can't feel anything from below the throb in your knees.

You work the worm with both hands. You roll it around the rod, pinch to hold it there, and turn like you're wrapping up a cord. You try going slow and then going hard and fast. The pain darkens your vision. You feel like you'll never be able to get up off your knees. You alternate, because neither method is better than the other, even though you think it might change. You try to ignore the watery blood dripping down your legs.

How long is it? How many inches have you already pulled out of yourself? You count the inches, estimating your progress:

Five, ten, fifteen, twenty, twenty-five, thirty, thirty-five....

"Counting Inches in the Emergency Room"

WILL CLEMENTS is an application developer from Indiana, in the United States. He's had success writing in many modalities — pad & paper, typewriter, computer screen — but these days he's taken to writing in Google Docs on his phone. It takes a lot of self-discipline, and can be tedious when thumbs are too slow for the brain, but it's a tool that is always at hand. "Counting Inches in the Emergency Room" is his first published story.

He says: "I wanted to try something experimental, something I've never done with a story before, hence the second person viewpoint. The tale is loosely based on a real-life experience with a blood clot (that looked like a blood-red worm when passed) while I was also dealing with a kidney stone."

Usha's Sarees

PLEASE, GOD, let him telephone me now.

As Usha waits in the headmaster's office for the call back from her father that would inform her that he is on his way, she is an anxious mess. The first time she had seen it, she couldn't help but be overcome with the faintest sense of panic. It hadn't been big, and it hadn't spread to the rest of her clothes, but it's still there.

A big, red-brown stain on her underclothes.

She knew it was coming — she was told as much by her grandmothers and aunts, who recounted stories of how the blood seeped through the whites and pale blues of their school uniforms, a permanent mark of their transition into womanhood. Even in school, she had started to hear whispers floating around among the girls in her class as if it was a forbidden secret, meant only to be locked away in the minds of women.

She just didn't think it would come so soon — the blood or the ending of her childhood. She doesn't know which it is, and mulls it over as she sits demurely in the back seat of her father's car when he picks her up from school. She is suddenly overcome with a sense of embarrassment and shame — *how could her father see her like this?* — as she feels a chasm beginning to open, a distance separating her from the man she admired so dearly.

She receives her first *saree* later that night from her mother as they talk in her room — green, to represent fertility, her mother tells her. It's a nice green — not the mottled, ugly kind she sees in some storefronts — a pale, airy color. But with each rustle of the stiff, satin-silk fabric as her mother wraps it around her too-skinny hips, she can feel the heavy constraints of womanhood sinking into her skin, tightening around her legs as it becomes difficult to move.

Swish. No more climbing trees to reach the mangoes hanging tantalizingly on the highest branch. *Swish.* No more running around with the neighborhood boys as they bathed in childhood joy. *Swish.* No more carefree games on dirt roads. *Swish.* Spending days in the kitchen cooking the perfect dal and roti and sabzi, so that she can practically feel the heat from the kitchen lodging itself in her bones. *Swish.* Hours learning to clean the dishes and pots and pans, and leaving long, draping yards of fabric to dry in the omnipresent heat of Nanded.

As she turns, she catches a glance of herself in the mirror. She looks like a painted doll, perfectly groomed and starched to be the next in line to inherit the role of a traditional woman. The only vestiges of girlhood that peek through the silken threads are the scars and scrapes from falling off of her bicycle and playing cricket in the streets.

Finally, her mother fastens the last safety pin in place as she drapes the remainder of the *saree* around her body.

You look beautiful, Usha, her mother whispers with pride gleaming in her eyes.

She musters up a nod of assent and a fleeting smile, the weight of the *pallu* permanently affixed to her left shoulder.

She receives the next *saree* at the *haldi* ceremony, just days before her wedding commences. The rituals of this particular event are familiar to her; she's attended enough weddings to understand that this may be the last time for the coming months, if not years, that she can savor the company of her closest friends and relatives by herself.

But her excitement quickly turns bittersweet when her

uncle begins applying the uptan paste on her face, the smell of sandalwood and turmeric suddenly throwing her into the past. She is reminded of lazy, laughter-laden summers saturated with sticky mango juice and ice cream, walks in the gardens and sunbeams bleaching the walls of the old house.

Opening her eyes, she glances at the people surrounding her: Naina, her childhood best friend, with whom she had traded books and notes and giggles and secrets; the uncles who had slipped her hard candies wrapped in crinkly cellophane and small 5-*rupee* coins; the aunties who had taught her that the secret ingredient in every recipe was always more *ghee*. Basking in the glow of affection of the keepers of her memories, she soaks in the voices of her childhood as they sear themselves into her mind.

She never wants to leave this behind.

Nevertheless, she tries not to let the tears spill over and ruin the makeup and turmeric plastered on her face as her uncle finally presses the packaged golden yellow *saree* into her hands.

Crossing the threshold with Amitabh, her newly minted husband, into the house in Mumbai for the first time, she is immediately overwhelmed by the unfamiliarity, forgetting, if only for a moment, that technically this house belongs to her too now. The door clicks shut behind them, as if it marks her final transition into adulthood, sealing her fate into this family.

Her new mother and father are sitting on the embroidered couch in the living room, talking softly to each other as they sip the cups of *chai* that Nanda, the cook whom Amitabh had told her about, must have prepared, based on the scents of ginger, cardamom, and lemongrass wafting through the house. Upon seeing them, Usha quickly crosses the room as briskly as she can, the *saree* restricting her strides into graceful, small steps, before bending down to touch the feet of her in-laws.

She remembers all the advice from her aunts and married cousins and mother, how she would have to adapt to her new family's rituals and customs, seamlessly blending into their culture.

Like sugar in warm water, her mother had said.

She keeps her head down as she approaches her mother-in-law, modest and shy in the presence of these two figures despite engaging in mindless revelry with them during the wedding. At last, her mother-in-law tilts up her chin and gives her a beaming smile.

Beti, I have a gift for you, she says.

A purple *saree,* the color of an eggplant, a rich, warm violet lays in her hands.

All at once, her apprehension dissolves, and for the first time, she no longer feels nervous in the presence of the family that bears her new last name.

It's only six months later, in October, that she finds herself in London with her husband, renting an apartment from an elderly Pakistani man. He is the only one who looks like them, a small comfort in this foreign, unknown land.

Diwali approaches with alarming rapidity. It's the first *Diwali* she's spent away from home, away from railings lined with hundreds of luminous *diyas,* porches decorated with *rangoli* patterns, endless plates of *kheer* and *rabdi* and *gulab jamuns* and *mithai,* so when Amitabh suggests that they attend the function that the local Indian Association is hosting at the hotel 10 blocks away, she doesn't hesitate before agreeing.

That evening, she wears the royal blue *saree* that her father had sent her, embroidered with gold and silver borders. It's one of the few items she owns from home, and didn't think she'd ever have an occasion for wearing it. Amitabh, too, has broken out his black *kurta* to match. It's a beautiful dusk, the last remains of sunlight still peeking through and warming the sidewalk, so they decide to walk to the venue.

But she is unprepared for the calculating looks from strangers, the ones from blue eyes that pierce her soul and make her squirm in her own skin, and she regrets stepping out at all. They're less than a block away from the hotel when a man behind her barks, *Fucking Paki* at her back. They don't know what direction it comes from, so they simply speed up without looking back, walking as fast as her *saree* will let her.

When they finally open the doors to the function, she feels somewhat more at ease, surrounded by the smell of fried samosas and curries. The words from the man keep bouncing around her brain like a bad record, though, and for the rest of the evening, all she can think of is *fucking Paki, fucking Paki, fucking Paki.*

They take a taxi back to their flat as Amitabh tightly grips her hand.

The *barsa* for her first daughter is busier than she had expected.

She knew it would be a big deal, especially since she and Amitabh had returned from England, but it doesn't stop the occasional moments of claustrophobia that threaten to overwhelm her senses, from the shouting of the guests to the clamoring of Tara in the bassinet to the smell of the buffet from the caterer floating through the open night air.

That evening, she wears the green and red *saree* that her mother-in-law gave her for this very occasion. In some ways, it reminds her of the first green *saree* that she got, yet another representation of her womanly fertility, but this time, it is not tainted with the shame that she experienced at 11 years old. Now, it shows her strength, how her body is able to create this child, full of giggles and lusty cries.

She is thankful, and lucky, that her husband wanted a girl, so unlike the husbands of her childhood friends.

Growing up, in her village, everyone celebrated the boys, handing out sweets and blessings, while the girls were relegated to the kitchen. She may have been born on August 15th, in the year of her homeland's independence, but tonight, noticing the love people shower her daughter with, she knows that there is a new kind of freedom that awaits Tara in her future.

As she watches him rock her daughter back and forth, soothing her wailing, a soft smile comes across her face as her fears dissipate and she gently fingers the edge of the embroidered *pallu*.

She doesn't get an opportunity to wear a new *saree* for another five years, while she and Amitabh reside in England as he finishes his Ph.D., a continent away from their Tara. In many ways, England has been kinder to her during this trip — she's found a small group of friends, with perfectly coiled blond curls and blue eyes who fawn over her simple *sarees* and homemade *dal* and rice. The gritty streets of Manchester have grown on her, their smell of petrichor and cement slowly worming their way into her soul.

Even still, she's thankful when Amitabh finally books their tickets for home (a small, cramped bungalow in Pune) on a rainy October evening as they lounge around in their flat.

She is wearing one of the *sarees* she picked up in England when she arrives on the doorstep of her home. It was somewhat of an impulsive purchase — she had been traversing the lanes of the Little India neighborhood as she had gone to get her weekly supply of tea leaves, spices, and *dal*, and had spotted the new *saree* shop that had suddenly cropped up between the grocery store and the jewelry store. It was a pretty peach chiffon — a lightweight, gossamer thing with delicate embroidery along the sides, little white flower petals. She hadn't had any occasion for wearing it while in England — the weather had been too cold for it to emerge from its plastic wrapping when the occasion actually arose. But it did fit perfectly with the humidity that had recently swamped Pune and Mumbai, as she realized when the warm breeze hit her face as she exited the plane.

Standing in front of their house, they hesitantly knock on the aged wooden panel, once, twice, three times, before the door swings open to reveal their five-year old daughter, with her grandparents — Amitabh's parents — standing behind her.

And then, smiles and laughter abound as she joyously swings her daughter around in her arms, pressing a kiss into her thick curls.

The next time she goes out to buy a *saree*, it is for the marriage of her first daughter.

The past few months have been so full of activity in preparation for the wedding, especially given that both Tara and her husband-to-be are still in the US, that she has barely taken any time for herself.

Today, however, her husband has taken her out to the new clothing shop a couple of streets away to buy her a new *saree* for the wedding ceremony. It feels like something out of a dream, as she saunters through the aisles filled with brightly patterned fabric.

It's the one she sees at the very back of the store, a rich red-maroon with a gold border, that she knows is the right one. The significance of the moment suddenly hits her as she stares at this *saree*: even though her daughter has already left for the US, this is a figurative transition, as Tara will soon adopt a new last name in a new home in a strange place, leaving them behind as she becomes part of her husband's family.

She shakes her head, clearing her mind of those thoughts. *It's a different time now*, she reminds herself. Tara will never feel the pressures from extended family or the burden to produce a boy, or know the intensive process to fit into the roles society dictates she must do. After all, she is studying her Master's degree in an American university, training to be an engineer.

But it doesn't make it any easier to let her go.

Amitabh glances over, taking note of the tears starting to pool in her eyes, and suddenly he's there, wrapping his arms around her, grounding her as he surrounds her with his warmth and familiarity.

And so they stand there in each other's embrace in the middle of the department store with watery smiles as they prepare to give away their first child.

It is six years later when she receives a call from Heathrow.

Are you Usha Joshi? the cold British voice on the other end asks. As she replies with a shaky *yes*, she can already feel the apprehension building in the pit of her stomach.

Your husband, Amitabh, died a little less than an hour ago.

Her world stops spinning after that. She can barely register what the attendant on the line is saying, catching phrases like "heart attack" and "doctors couldn't save him", and she collapses onto a chair. It feels like a surreal nightmare, like the floor beneath her has been swept away, and she feels as though she is suffocating on her own grief, on the lump in her throat.

It wasn't supposed to happen like this, not when he was 55, not in the middle of a European airport.

Her sister and mother come later that evening, bearing a simple white cotton *saree* for her to wear during the cremation. She is numb and in shock, and her blank face scares them more than her sobs ever could.

The ceremony happens two days later, when both of her daughters and their husbands have arrived, her eldest daughter's belly swollen from seven months of pregnancy. There is no time to mourn then, as she manages the hordes of people who have come to pay their respects to her husband, from childhood friends and classmates to employers and even a few people from their time in England. The anguish hangs heavy in the air, blanketing them with its weight, as she fights to get reprieve from the overwhelming sadness that surrounds and consumes her.

It is only after they finish pouring his ashes into the water by Juhu Beach that she returns home, and finally succumbs to her own tears.

A few days later, her family arrives, filling the echoing emptiness left in Amitabh's wake. She is worried that it will just be more crying, and she isn't sure if her soul can bear the combined weight of her misery and that of her family's.

But then, her sister-in-law makes a joke, recalling the time Amitabh stole ghee from the kitchen as a child, like baby *Krishna*, and for the first time in the days since the phone call, she laughs.

It is exactly one year and two months later that she's back in India, returning after months of spending time with her year-old granddaughter, Anushka. It's her granddaughter's naming ceremony this time, a generation later, and she feels a pang of emptiness, a twinge of loss striking her heart as she wishes Amitabh could be here to see the granddaughter he had known only in his daughter's belly.

There are some days she worries about Tara and Anushka, about their future in a place an ocean away. About whether or not Anushka will grow up knowing how to play cricket, or the taste of fresh *aamras*, or the myths of gods and goddesses and demons and sages that had defined her childhood. About whether or not she will know the intricacies of the language that were the sources of Usha's own memories.

She wonders if Anushka will ever get the chance to wear the *sarees* that have started to build up in her closet, or if she would bury herself solely in the clothes of her American friends. Whether she would wear *bindis* and *payal* and glittering *lehenga cholis*; whether Tara might dress her up in a green *saree* just as she was by her own mother all those years ago.

Darkness is falling on Pune, and she catches a glimpse of the stars twinkling, the ones that aren't obscured by the waves of fog rolling in over the city. And as night approaches, she watches the minute hand slip forward in five-minute increments, time careening towards a new future.

Five, ten, fifteen, twenty, twenty-five, thirty, thirty-five.

"Usha's Sarees"

NINA KAUSHIKKAR is a student from Illinois, in the United States. As the daughter of two Indian immigrants, her identity as an Indian-American woman heavily affects what she chooses to write about. "Usha's Sarees" is her first published story, and the winner of this year's Parker contest. We loved the way its contemplative narrator moved through time, and the simple conceit of telling her story through a length of silk. The interpretation of Parker's first and last lines was both bittersweet and beautiful. It was a delight to read and a pleasure to award.

She says: "I have loved reading from a young age, but I noticed that none of the stories I read mirrored my own background or experiences of Indian-American children growing up in America. At the encouragement of family members and teachers, I began writing the narratives that I yearned to hear. 'Usha's Sarees' is the product of my desire to share my heritage and my attempt to add to the broader tapestry of immigrant histories."

Nature Will Provide

PLEASE, GOD, let me him telephone me now.

Please.

Please.

Abigail stares at the phone; an old-fashioned rotary dial, its cord thick and frayed. The receiver weighs more than three iPhones combined. Still, it works. There was a dial tone when she picked it up; there was the *clickety-click-click* as numbers were dialed, painstakingly.

He didn't answer the phone. No one did.

She got his voicemail — at least she thinks it's his voicemail, the automated voice telling her to leave a message for his mailbox.

Did there used to be a greeting? She can't remember.

She left the message. Telling him to call. That she is where she is supposed to be.

And now she waits.

In this tiny cabin.

Whose idea was this? His idea. All of this.

I hope he's right, she thinks. And then: *Wait, do I?*

She shifts in the wooden chair, pushing it back, and it creaks beneath her. In front of her is the telephone table, supporting the ancient piece of black Bakelite, a phone book (last issued in 2008), and a yellowed pad, a pencil. On a small piece of laminated cardboard:

Welcome to Shady Woods Cabins!
We Hope You Enjoy Your Stay!

If At Any Time You Need Help,
Please Call the Management Office.

Remember, Always Extinguish All Fires,
Both Indoors or Out. Smokey Thanks You!

Beneath that, someone had drawn a fair representation of a bear in a ranger's hat.

She wonders where the other cabins are located. On the drive she hadn't seen a single structure, or person. Just miles and miles of woods down the end of a slim dirt road.

Her shoulders still ache from clenching the wheel as the little rental hit stump, stone, and hole, over and over.

Seriously, whose idea was this?

She turns from the telephone table and gets up, stretching her arms above her head. The ceilings are so low she can nearly skim it with her fingertips. And she is not tall. She lowers her arms and fluffs her hair, lifting to allow cool air at her neck.

The one-room cabin has not been used much in recent years; she expected this. He had told her as much when they made the plans. A brother's cousin's uncle told him about it. Or something. Abandoned. Useful to hunters, occasional hiker on the trail.

Don't worry, he'd said. *No one's going to come and yell at us. Especially when —*

She walks into the kitchen nook, noticing the dust feathering from the hanging skillet, pot. There is no refrigerator. Only a large belted cooler. She studies it; wonders what might be inside. She turns away. No stove, just a two-burner hot plate. No sink; instead, a hand pump. And no bathroom.

She's been avoiding it; avoiding thinking about it but now that she's here, finally, she knows she has to make some adjustments. There's an outhouse. He told her about it. And even if he hadn't she saw it when she pulled into the weed-choked driveway.

An outhouse.

She steps out the side door, onto the thin porch. It feels surprisingly sturdy under the heel of her boot. There's rocking chair in one corner, faded and sun-bleached. It looks like one strong breeze would blow it to kindling.

A rattling, above.

She looks up. Tucked in the rafters is a nest. Inside it, something peeps and scrambles.

She is sitting in the car, engine idling, charging her phone. She wasn't supposed to keep it with her, according to the plan, but in the rush she guesses she forgot. She guesses, but she knows she didn't, not really.

But there is no signal; she knew there wouldn't be. He'd warned her; but still she figures it won't hurt to check again. Now and then. Until the car is out of gas, anyway.

The phone turns on; searches, searches, searches. Nothing. She is off the grid.

She is alone.

Whose idea was this?

She sits in the rocking chair, slowly tilting back and forth, watching a line of ants moving down the porch railing. She counts them: *one, two, three....*

It's been a week. One week and he hasn't called. Hasn't fucking called.

One week and she hasn't seen anyone. *Heard* anyone.

She rocks, thinking. So far, there is enough food. That at least has gone according to plan. Nothing exciting but she could do worse than canned beans, tomato soup. She'll be all right for another few weeks, even without skimping.

The well water is cold, pure, and sweet. She's not sure

she ever tasted water like that back home.

She'll live. For a time.

She's managed the outhouse. There is even a small supply of toilet paper. This, she thinks, will be the first thing to go. A leaf blows past her foot, brushing against the column of ants, and she smiles. *Yes, well, nature will provide.* She laughs, loud.

Still, it's August. Fall is creeping in at night. She can feel it now, even though the afternoon sun is high and bright. There, at the breeze's edge; autumn.

After that it's winter. What then?

She thinks of the gun. It was the first thing she looked for, that second day, after a restless, dreamless night on the musty cot. She knew there'd be one; they planned for it, but she wanted to be sure. If he was going to take a long time coming, she needed to know where it was, and how to use it.

For dinner that night, she has rabbit stew. She still has a few weeks of canned goods but she figured when she saw the fat rabbit sitting blindly on the hood of her car that she might as well test her hand at hunting. Turns out, she is a surprisingly good shot.

In the mornings, now, after she awakes, heats water for her tea (an endless supply it seems), she sits by the black corded phone and marks the day on the faded memo pad. Like a prisoner in the oubliette, she scratches a line. Counts them out. Except her sentence is indeterminate; her time in the hole without end. Still it helps to keep track. It's been, by her accounting, thirty-four days. It's mid-September or thereabouts. The nights come cooler and quicker now; her supply of firewood is alarmingly low. There is an ax, there are trees. She supposes she will learn to make do.

After the accounting, she picks up the heavy receiver and slowly dials the number. *Clickety-click-click.* She listens to the computer voice tell her to leave a message. Sometimes she does; usually she does not.

And then she drinks her tea.

The snow falls in wide fat flakes, like the ashes of burnt paper. She stands at the window, watching, mesmerized.

She thinks it might be Christmas. She isn't sure precisely but it is near enough. She lowers her head and prays thanks to the infant Jesus.

Two things:

One, the phone is dead. Not her phone, *his*. When she calls this morning there is no automated answer, just a click and static. It's the first change aside from the seasons.

Two, she has run out of matches. The fire, always banked or roaring depending on time of day, must now never be allowed to go out.

She looks at the pad: it is nearing March, spring. When the snow clears; she is going to drive the car back down the road until the gas runs out. And then she will walk. She will walk and walk and walk until she finds something. Anything. She cannot stay here.

June, or close to it. The skies are blue, the sun shines. She found a patch of wild strawberries in a small glade. She pet a fawn as it lay curled in the grass waiting its mother. She stole tiny eggs from a bird's nest and cracked them into her mouth.

She sleeps outside most nights now. She wears few clothes. Why bother? There is no one. There is nothing. This is her world and she is free.

The phone rings. At first the sound is so loud, so discordant, she thinks she is hallucinating again; like she first thought she heard the frogs talking about her, when in reality they were talking to her. Or the crows and their loud secrets.

Bringggggggggggg. Bringggggggggggg.

It causes the tiny table to tremble with the force of its bell. She stares at it, mesmerized. Her heart beating hard against her ribs.

She realizes what she is supposed to do: *Answer it!* in some distant part of her brain, but it feels far off, removed. *Answer it answer it answer it answer it.* She steps closer.

Bringggggggggggg. Bringggggggggggg. Bringggggggggggg.

She reaches a tentative hand toward it, retreats. *Answer it! Answer it! Answer it! Answer it!* — She flees out the back door and runs and runs and runs.

She is completely naked. Her hair, all of it, wild and thick, like a mountain lamb, unshorn. Around her crown she has made a garland of wildflowers, thorns, a pine cone, a rabbit bone. It rattles as she walks through the woods, rifle on her shoulder.

The phone has not rung again. Instead it is in pieces in the stream, smashed to bits and left to assimilate back into the real world.

She walks. She has mapped these woods in her mind, she can circle around and back without getting lost, always finding the cabin, her glade.

She also found one other cabin, abandoned, half-caved in, a tree growing up its middle. Inside, through one of the black window holes she saw the outline, the shape, of a telephone.

The air is growing cooler again. Slightly. She can smell it in the air, as she sits, on the porch, gun across her lap.

And then, a droning. A *hum*. From down the road. Is it? What is —

She stands. Readies the gun at her shoulder.

A *car* rolls into view. It is moving slowly, purposefully. It stops abruptly in front of her cabin. The door opens, a man practically falls out. He is thin, his face gutted with loss.

"Abigail?" he cries out.

She cocks the gun. Fires.

The ants continue to march down the porch railing. She watches them, rocks in her chair, and counts.

Five, ten, fifteen, twenty, twenty-five, thirty, thirty-five.

"Nature Will Provide"

JUSTINE GARDNER is a freelance copyeditor from Brooklyn, New York. In addition to writing, she enjoys taking pictures of abandoned toilet bowls and posting them on Instagram under @toilet_town. "Nature Will Provide" is her first published story.

She says: "The urgency of the opening Parker line immediately brought to mind a scene of a young woman, waiting for a phone call — but not in the usual sense. The entire story came out in a one-hour sitting and I barely had time to make it coherent before sending it in for consideration."

Appendix 1

Honorable Mentions

We received nearly one thousand submissions to this year's Literary Taxidermy Short Story Competition, and many impressed both early readers and final judges. In the end some good stories were turned away. The following stories all made it to the last round of selection. Keep an eye out for these writers. We're confident you'll see their work in the future.

Yomn Alkhazaali, "-31.5"
Amy Bojang, "All at Sea"
Corina Clancy, "Call Me Cleopatra"
Cathy Day, "Forever A Part"
Essie Dee, "Working with Numbers"
Olivia Edwards, "Beloved Significant Other"
Sean Fallon, "Sext"
Dorothy Faulk and Marianne Nicol, "The Calling"
Deb y Felio, "New York, New York"
Lara Haynes Freed, "Belonging"
Ana Gardner, "The Recursion Problem"
Abigail Verity Graham, "The Trumpet"
Emily Hanlon, "Reunion"
Kirsten Irving, "The Tombola"
Samantha Johnson, "The Jellybean Bet"
Molly S. Kelash, "Death by Numbers"
Bethany King, "Silence"

Rachele Krivichi, "In the Shop"
Carol June Martin, "Pub People"
Lynn Maver, "The Whole Picture"
Rachelle Longé McGhee, "Femme Fatale"
D. A. Madigan, "Parker"
Charlene Mertz, "Thanksalot"
Skylar Nitzel, "Frozen Time"
Kierri Price, "Arithmomania"
Elaine Ricci, "A Dark Obsession"
Sierra B. Ryan, "Before Texting"
Vinnie Sarrocco, "Last Moments of Velma Barfield"
Danielle Sepulveres, "Girls Interrupted"
Jennifer Smith, "Naxos"
Sierra Smith, "The Consequences of Ignoring the Rain"
Bryan Teague, "What Is in Front of You"
D. J. Tyrer, "Inspection"

This Year's Judges

Given the eclectic nature of the three opening/closing lines in the 2018 Literary Taxidermy Short Story Competition, and our desire for submissions to span genres, we assembled a group of professional writers and editors from all walks of the literary life. The judges for this year's competition included a poet, a playwright, a mystery writer, a speculative fiction writer, a fantasy writer, a young adult writer, a horror writer, and a food writer. They had a challenging task, separating not only wheat from chaff, but wheat from wheat, and we are grateful for their enthusiastic and perspicacious participation.

Catherine Barnett is the author of three collections of poems: *Human Hours* (2018), *The Game of Boxes* (2012), and *Into Perfect Spheres Such Holes Are Pierced* (2004). Her honors include a Whiting Award, a Guggenheim Fellowship, and the James Laughlin Award from the Academy of American Poets. She has published widely in journals and magazines, including *The New Yorker*, *The Kenyon Review*, and *The Washington Post*. Barnett teaches in the graduate and undergraduate programs at New York University, is a distinguished lecturer at Hunter College. She has degrees from Princeton University, where she has taught in the Lewis Center for the Arts, and from the MFA Program for Writers at Warren Wilson College.

Kelley Eskridge is a fiction writer, essayist, and screenwriter. She is the author of the New York Times

Notable novel *Solitaire*, a finalist for the Nebula, Endeavour, and Spectrum awards. The short stories in her collection *Dangerous Space* include an Astraea prize winner and finalists for the Nebula and Tiptree awards. Eskridge's story "Alien Jane" was adapted for an episode of the SciFi channel series Welcome to Paradox. Her film *OtherLife* (2017) is currently streaming on Netflix. She is a former vice president of Wizards of the Coast, the company responsible for the collectible trading games *Magic*™ and *Pokémon*™. She earns her keep as a corporate learning professional, as well as an independent editor with an international client list of established and emerging writers. She lives in Seattle with her wife, novelist Nicola Griffith.

Stephen Graham Jones is a Blackfeet author of experimental fiction, horror fiction, crime fiction, and science fiction. He has published in everything from literary journals to truck-enthusiast magazines, from textbooks to anthologies to best-of-the-year annuals. Jones has been an NEA Fellow, a Texas Writers League Fellow, and has won the Texas Institute of Letters Award for Fiction and the Independent Publishers Multicultural Award. His areas of interest, aside from fiction writing, are horror, science fiction, fantasy, film, comic books, pop culture, paleoanthropology, technology, and American Indian Studies. Jones received his BA in English and Philosophy from Texas Tech University (1994), his MA in English from the University of North Texas (1996), and his PhD from Florida State University (1998).

Holly Kowitt has written more than fifty books for younger readers, including *The Fenderbenders Get Lost in America*, *This Book Is a Joke*, *This Dance is Doomed*, and *The Principal's Underwear is Missing* (a brilliant update of PG Wodehouse's *Jeeves and Wooster*, set in a suburban high school). She also wrote and illustrated the bestselling LOSER LIST series, which has been translated into ten languages. She grew up in Evanston, Illinois and graduated from Brown University. A former editor at Scholastic Books, she lives in New York City, where she enjoys cycling, flea markets, and West Coast swing dancing. She spends most days writing and drawing in her art studio in Harlem.

Brian Parks is an American playwright, journalist, and editor. He lives in New York City and served as the Arts & Culture editor at *The Village Voice*, as well as Chairman of the Obie Awards. As a playwright, Brian has produced works that are noted for their dark comedy and fast pace. Best known for his play "Americana Absurdum" (which consists of the two shorter plays, "Vomit & Roses" and "Wolverine Dream"), his other works include "Goner," "Suspicious Package," "Out of the Way," "The Invitation," and "Imperial Fizz." "Americana Absurdum" was honored with the Best Writing award at the 1997 New York International Fringe Festival and a Scotsman Fringe First Award at the 2000 Edinburgh Festival Fringe. He is currently Senior Editor at *4Columns*, a website of arts criticism aimed at a general audience.

Michael Pronko is a mystery writer, essayist, and teacher, born in Kansas City, but living and writing in Tokyo for the past twenty years. He has published three award-winning collections of essays: *Beauty and Chaos: Essays on Tokyo*; *Motions and Moments: More Essays on Tokyo*; and *Tokyo's Mystery Deepens*. His award-winning mystery novel *The Last Train* (and the forthcoming *Thai Girl in Tokyo* and *Japan Hand*) feature Detective Hiroshi Shimizu who investigates white collar crime in Tokyo. He writes regularly for many publications, including *The Japan Times*, *Newsweek Japan*, *Jazznin*, *Jazz Colo[u]rs*, and *Artscape Japan*; and runs his own website, *Jazz in Japan*. He is a professor of American Literature at Meiji Gakuin University where he teaches seminars in contemporary novels and film adaptations.

Becky Selengut is a cooking teacher, private chef, not-so-private comedian, and a prolific food writer. Her books include *The Washington Local and Seasonal Cookbook* (2008); *Good Fish: Sustainable Seafood Recipes from the Pacific Coast* (2011 and 2018); *Shroom: Mind-Bendingly Good Recipes for Cultivated and Wild Mushrooms* (2014); *Not One Shrine: Two Food Writers Devour Tokyo* (2016); and *How to Taste: The Curious Cook's Handbook to seasoning and balance, from umami to acid and beyond* (2018). In her spare time she co-hosts Look Inside This Book Club, a NSFW comedy podcast with Matthew Amster-Burton that discusses the free Kindle preview — and ONLY the preview — of bestselling books, usually while sipping Pinot Grigio.

Nisi Shawl is an African-American writer, editor, and journalist. She is best known as an author of fantasy and science fiction who writes and teaches about how fantastic fiction might reflect real-world diversity of gender, sexual orientation, race, colonialism, physical ability, age, and other sociocultural factors. Her debut novel, *Everfair*, was a 2016 Nebula Awards finalist, and her short stories have appeared in *Asimov's Science Fiction*, the *Infinite Matrix*, *Strange Horizons*, *Semiotext(e)* and numerous other magazines and anthologies. Her story collection Filter House was one of two winners of the 2008 James Tiptree, Jr. Award. During the ceremony, she was crowned with the Tiptree tiara and given a plaque, a check, a pie, and a ceramic sculpture of a duck.

You, Too, May Become a Taxidermist!

All of us at Regulus Press wish to extend our thanks and appreciation to everyone who participated in this year's Literary Taxidermy Short Story Competition. Your enthusiasm and commitment far exceeded our expectations — as did the *overwhelming* number of story submissions we received for each contest.

If you didn't participate this year and are coming to this collection of stories new to the idea of literary taxidermy, we hope you've enjoyed what you've found. And if you're a writer, we encourage you — the present reader — to become a future author.

Regulus Press plans to host another literary taxidermy competition, and we're looking for writers, both amateur and professional, to stitch together new and imaginative stories. The competition is your chance to get your hands dirty and join the growing community of literary taxidermists.

For the latest on the competition (and to learn more about the possibilities of literary taxidermy), visit:

www.literarytaxidermy.com

We all look forward to seeing what you come up with!

About the Editor

Mark Malamud is principal and manager of busymonster, LLC, a consultancy company focused on advanced user interface and design. His collection of short stories, *The Gymnasium*, established the idea of literary taxidermy. His novel, *Float the Pooch*, which pits David Bowie against Stanley Kubrick against a background of alien invasion, future sex, and Yom Kippur, is widely unread. He holds over 700 patents, and in 2012 he was the 8th most-prolific inventor of patents in the US. His current interests include shearing, obscure knights, alternate endings, and vowels.

Other Books from Regulus Press

One Thing Was Certain

An anthology of literary taxidermy based on the first and last lines of *Through the Looking-Glass* by Lewis Carroll. Award-winning stories from the 2018 Literary Taxidermy Short Story Competition.

Against the Bar

An anthology of literary taxidermy based on the first and last lines of *The Thin Man* by Dashiell Hammett. Award-winning stories from the 2018 Literary Taxidermy Short Story Competition.

A Pocketful of Fish

An omnibus collection of poetry from North America's "most redoubtable poet." Includes the complete *Swimming through the Darkness* (1974), *Roe Roe Roe Your Boat* (1978), and *Will You Hold My Breath* (1994). Ichthyic poems by Choo 3T Fish.

Float the Pooch

Disco Rigido, charismatic kingpin of black-market libidinal software, spreads mayhem throughout the world for the benefit of an ancient extraterrestrial intelligence that uses life on Earth as a substrate for procreation; while Doctor Memory, a back-alley neurosurgeon dressed as a rabbi, tries to save what's left of humanity. A novel by Mark Malamud.